The Woodcutter

The Woodcutter

KATE DANLEY

47NORTH

Text copyright © 2010 Kate Danley

First 47North edition, 2012

Published by 47North

P.O. Box 400818

Las Vegas, NV 89140

ISBN-13: 9781612185408

ISBN-10: 1612185401

To my family

CHAPTER 1

The darkness settled like wings, blocking out the sun and casting the forest into false night. A woman no older than sixteen ran through the trees, her white ball gown of gossamer gathered in her hands.

The leaves shivered in the wind and whispered a warning. *Quietly! Quietly!* they spoke. Though she could not understand their words, her breath caught in her throat, for she heard the clatter of death waiting to fall.

The Beast was nearing.

The earth tried to soften the ground as she flew, to muffle her feet in moss and mud, but it was not quite quiet enough.

She exhaled and the cold darkness overcame her. With fangs of ice, the wind bit and gnawed at the very marrow of her bones. It yanked her strawberry curls from atop her head and wrapped them around her swan-like neck. It spat clods of mud at her eyes until she could not see. She stopped, frozen in place, knowing there was no escape. All that was left was to turn and face the Beast.

And in that terrible moment, though her body chose to fight the monster that was stalking her, her soul refused such a death and leapt from her body to continue its flight.

The husk of her flesh fell silently to the forest floor as her spirit ran on toward a doorway of light that appeared before her. Her spirit ran as she heard the footfalls fast behind her and as the cold wind became warm breath. Her feet were still moving as the Beast inhaled. Her scream still echoed as she clawed toward the light.

But the Beast inhaled again and her ghost halted in its tracks.

One final time he inhaled and her soul disappeared into his maw, no more than a wisp of smoke.

The forest was silent as the Beast padded away.

CHAPTER 2

A man knelt by the body and laid down his ax. The girl looked almost as if she were asleep, but her skin was too pale and the blue tinge to her lips gave her secret away.

He brushed aside a long red lock that was masking her delicate features. She was no one he knew, but the relief he felt was tempered with the knowledge that a stranger killed in this place was far worse. He picked up her arms and tilted her face. She was so young, so frail and light. His hands seemed clumsy and too large as he scanned her body for clues of her death. He found no signs of struggle. Only her white ball gown and chipped glass slippers suggested that she did not plan to lose herself in the Wood.

The man rocked back on his heels and looked up at the trees, knowing that they would be of no help. The sight of his ax had silenced their voices, even though his ax had never been tainted by sap. Those in this place did not know his purpose— his purpose, as had been his father's purpose, and his father's before that...

They did not know what it meant to be the Woodcutter.

He took a deep breath and let his eyelids fall to half-mast. The warmth came, gathered up from the earth, and channeled through him as smooth as a warm spring over a river rock. His vision blurred and he reached out to touch the girl.

Like lightning, a shock ran through his body. His heart convulsed and he choked back the cry wanting to tear itself roughly from his throat.

The taint of fear was like black tar upon the surface of a pond. She had been frightened, frightened to death, and her spirit had leapt from her body to try to save itself.

"Whatever did you get yourself into, child?" he whispered.

The Woodcutter wiped his hands upon his trousers and set about the grim duty of laying her to rest before the wolves found her.

CHAPTER 3

The Woodcutter opened the door to a small thatched home. A woman looked up from her cutting board, the staccato sound of chopping vegetables pausing as she brushed back a wisp that had escaped her tidy bun. Her gaze lingered upon him long enough to release the breath he did not know he was holding. He felt himself fall into the depths of her smile. She was a woman who had stood beside him for ten years and ten years more, and she was still the most beautiful woman he had ever seen.

"Wife," he greeted quietly as he walked to the hearth and sat to pull off his boots. The warmth of the fire seeped through his clothes, but today it could not chase away the chill of the girl in glass slippers.

His wife's wide hips rustled her skirt as she walked to the mantel and removed a small, carved box, just as she had every night for ten years and ten years more, and placed it on the table beside him. She laid a hand upon his shoulder. Like an old, gray-muzzled dog, the Woodcutter leaned against her, wanting nothing more than the peace brought by her touch. One might have thought she had a bit of the fae in her, but he knew better. Her spirit would not have been able to rest so quietly with him if the fae had mingled with her ancestors. She was who she was, no more, no less, and that was what made her so special.

She stroked his hair and then went back to her work.

He pulled his pipe from the box and lit the tobacco. The smoke wreathed his head, its wafting trails dancing to the music of the house, the music of stews boiling and tarts being taken from the oven. All else was silent as the minutes slowly ticked themselves comfortably away.

"Wife," he finally spoke.

She looked up.

"I shall have to leave," he said.

A slight tensing in her neck was the only betrayal that his words would keep her awake every night scanning the road for his safe return.

"When?" she asked so calmly it would put a player to shame, but he knew her tells.

The Woodcutter looked into the rings of smoke. They never lied.

"Tomorrow," he replied.

She nodded and took plates from the cupboard. "I shall prepare your things for the morning."

Their eyes locked, but neither of them spoke another word.

Indeed, the Woodcutter thought, never had a man loved a woman more.

CHAPTER 4

The lark welcomed the sun as the Woodcutter stretched in his bed. He could hear his wife stirring the coals downstairs. He rose and walked to the washbasin, splashing its cold water upon his face. It was a harsh greeting for the day. He wiped his dripping beard and looked out the window. Winter was fading and the tender touch of spring had caressed the earth, leaving its gift of new blossoms in delicate green.

He pulled his jerkin over his shoulders as he entered the main room. His wife greeted him with a kiss to the cheek and steered him to the table, knowing he would leave without breakfast if given a chance.

"I have placed food for two weeks in your pack and have filled two skins with water," she said as he sat.

He forked the eggs she had lovingly prepared and shoveled them into his mouth. He did not want to say that which must come next, but the words came as if bewitched from his lips.

"I shall need the velvet bag from the cupboard."

The plate slipped from his wife's fingers and crashed to the ground.

She hurriedly crouched to pick up the pieces, careful to mask the concern from her voice. "The black bag?"

"The black bag," he repeated, the words sounding calmer than he felt.

She threw the broken pottery into the rubbish bin. "Is it so terrible?"

He grunted, not daring to say more. The words they had spoken already could have been picked up by the wind and carried to ears that should not hear. The magic was too strong in the Wood.

His wife sighed, wiping her plain hands on her apron before opening the cupboard. She moved with strength and deliberation.

His wife had not known his calling before she married him. The first time he saw her was at the harvest festival. The absence of glamour was intoxicating. Surrounded by the swirl of other ladies in painted fineries and magicked perfumes, she stood in the firelight with no auras, no spells—just quiet, like an ancient oak rooted deep to the center of the earth.

His heavy feet carried him to her side as if by flight, and he had asked her to dance before he knew what he was doing.

She answered with a smile, a smile that revealed the clever wit beneath that silent face.

He had been taught since childhood to listen for answers in the gentle murmurs of a breeze. As he led her to the floor, he read her heart in the quickening of her breath, in the pressure of her fingers upon the crook of his arm, in the way her eyes sparkled in the lantern light. They said things he knew her lips never would.

And he knew, in that moment, he would never meet another woman like her if he traveled every inch of the world and back again.

They were wed before spring.

They were childless, as all Woodcutters are. His son had not yet found him, but blood would call blood. A child would be laid at their doorstep, and that child would grow to take over his role.

The Woodcutter watched his wife as she carefully placed the small bag within his traveling pack. He couldn't help the thought that danced across his mind: such a woman, who had waited ten years and then ten years more, should be allowed to have a child.

And with that unbidden musing came the blanket of failure. The child had not yet appeared, and the truth was that the Wood had not yet deemed them worthy parents. It had not yet deemed him a worthy father, for his wife was everything a child could ever want in a mother, and more.

"I have tucked the bag in the side pocket," she said, interrupting his sad reflection.

He rose from his seat, his breakfast eaten.

His wife walked him to the door and settled the straps upon his shoulders. "You will be careful, and you will return to me as soon as you can. I shall watch the moon and wait, my love."

He kissed her dearly and, with a final look, walked out into the morning mist.

CHAPTER 5

The Woodcutter sat by the deep water as it rushed by. He opened up his pack and placed his lunch upon the grass. There was a time and a place for movement, and the wind had whispered, *Hush*.

So the Woodcutter sat by the riverbank and finished his journey cake to the last crumb before the wind gave him leave to begin.

He took an onion from his pack. Carefully cutting it, he rubbed its juice across his hands and then moved to the water's edge. His hands unstrapped the ax at his side, an ax that was owned by his father and his father before him. He leaned over and listened to the water, listened to its gentle words as it guided him along. He listened and waited for the build to reach a crescendo.

And then he casually allowed the ax to fall.

"Oh, my ax! My ax!" he cried, wiping his eyes with his onion-laced fingers. As they burned, he made sure his tears fell into the river.

"Honest woodcutter, why do you cry?"

He looked up. A wrinkled old man with white whiskers and beady eyes sat in the fast current as relaxed and calm as if resting in a washbasin.

The Woodcutter felt the magic shape the words that came out of his lips: "I have lost my ax in the river, and without my ax, I shall not be able to cut wood for my family. Without wood for my family, my wife will surely die."

There was a gleam in the River God's eye.

"Why, honest woodcutter, I would be happy to fetch your ax from the river. Wait here and I will be naught but a moment," said the god.

The Woodcutter sat. The wind blew the hair on the back of his neck the wrong way.

The River God bobbed back to the surface. In his hand was an Ax of Shining Silver with green emeralds along the handle.

"Here you are, woodcutter. I have brought you your Ax."

The Woodcutter looked at the Ax and felt a strange warmth settle in his bones. It was the warmth of good memories and the notes of a beloved song. His eyes fell upon the emeralds.

Woodcutter, they whispered.

He could not tear himself away.

Woodcutter, the enchanted emeralds seemed to say. *Think of the comforts that just one of our stones could buy. Look at this silver. Think how it could be melted down and made into a necklace for your wife. Oh, how her eyes would sparkle; oh, how her face would light with joy.*

But his wife was plain and ordinary, he thought. She would laugh at him if he should even try to present her with such a gift.

Woodcutter, the emeralds enticed.

He thrust aside their call with a violent presence of will. "I am sorry, I am afraid that is not my ax."

The River God's face broke into a disappointed frown. "Are you quite sure?"

The Woodcutter shook his head wearily. "Indeed, that one is too fine for me."

The River God dove back down to the bottom of the water.

The Woodcutter wiped a cold sweat from his upper lip.

The River God came to the surface again. In his hand was an Ax of Gleaming Gold studded in rubies.

"This is the only other Ax I have found."

The Woodcutter swallowed. The rubies were the color of passion. *Such passion*, they promised, *and such love they could bring him. Red is your wife's favorite color. A golden comb with red rubies to pull back her hair. If you were a loving husband*, the rubies hissed, *you would seek out pretty pleasantries for a wife as good as yours.*

But he thought of his wife with rubies in her hair as she kneaded the bread and tended the fire. He clung to that image. His wife was simple and pure, he thought, and silenced the rubies' call.

He shook his head. "I am sorry, kind sir. But that too is not my ax."

The River God's teeth ground together, the sound of jagged bone against bone loud enough to be heard over the current. "Are you quite sure?" he asked.

The Woodcutter nodded.

The River God said nothing, but dove once more beneath the surface.

The River God returned, this time with an Ax of Pure Platinum encrusted in diamonds.

"Here you are. I have brought you your Ax."

Woodcutter, the diamonds sang, and their song felt like drowning. *Woodcutter, think of our strength, of our use. We can cut through any material.* The diamonds glinted in the sun. *Wouldn't your dear, sweet wife like a gift she could use?*

They pointed at their platinum. The Woodcutter could not breathe gazing upon the beauty.

Look, we shall never tarnish. How happy your wife would be for this gift.

He could feel his wife throw her arms around him, feel her hands in his hair and her breath warm upon his neck. She gazed into his eyes and whispered in the diamond's voice, *With just one diamond, I would never have to slave in the cottage one more day. With just one diamond, I could live like a queen.*

The Woodcutter drew in a ragged gasp and tried to gather thoughts of his wife, of her smiling face in the garden, grinning up at the sunflowers towering overhead. He thought of her in the deepest night, curled beside the fire to feed a young kitten that had been left by its mother too soon. She was humble and wise and knew how the world worked as it did. She would not wish to live like a queen. And though the diamonds called *Woodcutter,* he shook his head a third time and said, "I am sorry, I am afraid that Ax is not my own."

The River God's eyes flashed dangerously. "Are you quite sure?"

"Indeed, you are most kind, but this Ax is not my own."

The River God disappeared once more.

The Woodcutter swallowed, his breath tight in his ribs.

The River God returned and in his hand was the humble ax the Woodcutter had dropped.

"Oh, kind sir, you have found my ax!" the Woodcutter exclaimed.

A rumble of thunder sounded overhead. The River God roared in anger. "Since you are so honest and were guided by truth and not greed, all three Axes shall be yours."

The Woodcutter stood.

Many times, river gods would quietly hand over such gifts, but this god seemed to have played the game before.

The Woodcutter ducked as the plain ax spun toward his heart. He moved again as the Platinum Ax whizzed by his head. He leapt as the Gold Ax narrowly missed his shoulder and the Silver Ax sped at his knees.

The River God disappeared beneath the water, steam marking his exit as the surface boiled with his fury.

The Woodcutter picked up his father's ax and held it tightly for just a moment before placing it safely in his pack.

His hands trembled.

The ax was his birthright. Its humble iron head and plain oak handle held more power than any crown. Without his father's ax, there would be no more gifts from river gods. Without his father's ax, no son would ever find him. Without his father's ax, the Wood would claim him.

He tied the Gold and Platinum Axes together and stowed them away. He strapped the Silver Ax to his side and continued on in a direction far from the river's bank.

CHAPTER 6

He saw a flash of blonde between the trees and then her cape.

Red. Red as dark cherries.

He knew she should not be in the Wood. The child crouched in the clearing, gathering flowers in her arms.

"Small One?"

She turned, startled by his voice.

"Small One, you should not be here in the Wood all alone."

The Woodcutter had played his role in this story more than once. Sometimes he had been able to save the small one in the red cape. Sometimes he had not.

The faces of those children still haunted his dreams.

His senses prickled and he inhaled deeply, trying to catch the smell of whatever was watching. He knew the creature in this reenactment might be quite different than the others.

Glass slippers upon the blue-veined feet...

He looked at the sky. The creatures he knew most mortals should fear only came out at night, and there were still nine hours until darkness fell.

"You must leave the Wood," he said.

The little girl looked up at him with such wide blue eyes. "But my grandmother is sick, and I am bringing her food to make her well."

Her gaze felt like an afternoon sunbeam. This was no ordinary child. He could see the touch of the fae in the glow of her skin and the twinkle of her eyes. She seemed somehow more interesting than other people. It was the faerie glamour. Its royal blue blood beat within her human veins.

He tried to smile with reassurance. "You must hurry to her side, then. Stop to talk to no one."

She nodded at him in serious understanding and dropped a curtsy.

Not yet seven years old, he thought as he watched her dance away. Some of the older ones could fight off the wolves that seemed so drawn to young flesh.

His heart seemed to die with each tripping footstep she made farther and farther away from him.

He had to wait until she was out of sight before he followed. Such were the laws when mixed mortals wandered into his Wood. He could guide and protect, but not interfere. If the spirit of the fae beat within a mortal's veins, occasionally one of those people was merely a foolish soul who had mistakenly wandered into the Wood. He hoped it was such with the Small One in the red cloak.

Unfortunately, sometimes, they had been called home for a reason.

CHAPTER 7

The Woodcutter arrived at the house. The door was ajar.

As it always was.

His heart pounded. He knew what would face him when he entered the house, and braced himself for the wolf. He did not smell the foul reek of canine beast or the metallic tang of spilled blood. He hoped it meant that the battle had not yet begun.

Ordinary widows, the red-blooded elderly women of the Twelve Kingdoms, were drawn to the Wood in a way he could not understand. They built homes beneath the trees, seemingly anxious to take advantage of the forest's bounty. The truth was they came to the Wood to die. It was as if they were playing out a part in a story and the Wood had an insatiable appetite for that particular book. As soon as one grandmother perished, another moved into the home not days after the first disappeared.

It was his duty, as had been his father's duty and his father's father's duty before that, to slay the wolves that preyed upon them and their grandchildren, but even so, the Woodcutter cursed silently as he loosed the Silver Ax from his side. Usually he could have used his father's ax, but this child was special and the rules were different. This child was part fae with blue blood in her veins. She was the stock of royalty, and only a River God's Ax would do.

He had three opportunities to dispatch whatever evil had left the redheaded girl dead in the forest, three opportunities before he would have to return to the River God for more Axes. Now, one chance would be wasted because a mother sent her child into the Wood all alone and a grandmother did not fear child-eating wolves.

He crept up the stairs.

And then stopped.

The Small One was sprawled unnaturally upon the ground, her tumble of blonde curls spilled upon the wooden floor. Her tiny hand barely clutched her bouquet. The flowers that had escaped scattered across the slats as if in flight.

The grandmother sat in her bed, her face startled.

They were both most decidedly dead.

The air was thick with the tainted smell of fear, but there was not a wolf to slay in sight.

CHAPTER 8

He shut the door to the cottage quietly behind him.

There had been no wolf.

And a child was dead.

It was his duty to find the Small One's mother and tell her the news, find her so that she could lay both her mother and child to rest.

But he had failed in his most sacred duty, his duty, as had been his father's duty and his father's father's duty before that. In broad daylight, he had failed.

*There had been no wolf and the half-fae child was dead...*His feet seemed to walk to the rhythm of his failure.

He arrived in the village before dusk. There was only one place the type of mother who would send a half-fae child out to the Wood in a red cloak would live, a mother too busy eating toadstools or snorting pixie dust to care about the dangers found amidst the trees. The children of such mothers were forced to be adults long before their time.

He stepped into the brothel and a hush fell over the crowd. He made his way to a barkeeper, a burly man with one eye, and placed a wooden coin upon the counter.

"I am looking for a woman in this town who has a daughter, perhaps seven years in age. Blonde haired. Curls."

The barkeeper pushed the coin back toward him. "Woodcutter, your money is no good here." He called out to the backside of a stout woman, "Help this man."

The Madam turned. Her worn dress dipped dangerously in the front, revealing her aged and wrinkled breasts. She sashayed across the floor, faded burgundy skirts swaying from side to side. "Happy to."

She swallowed a large mouthful from her tankard and stepped close, fingering the Woodcutter's hooded Silver Ax. "And what can I do for a fine gentleman such as yourself?"

He looked into her blurry eyes. "I'm looking for a woman with a daughter about seven."

She swayed and leered at him. "So, you like the young ones, do you? Sick bastard."

He took a deep breath and risked waving his hand.

The wind from the Wood whispered, *Hush.*

But the small bit of magic was enough to raise the veil of the Madam's intoxication…just enough.

"I am looking for a woman with a daughter about seven, a woman who has a mother out in the Wood."

She stiffened. "The Wood?"

He nodded.

Her eyes nervously fell upon the silver handle at his waist. "Is that an Ax?"

He nodded once again.

She placed her cup upon the counter gently. "Follow me."

CHAPTER 9

The mother lay dressed in purple, sprawled out across the pillows. Her face was clouded with too much magic, and her body rolled in the seduction of faerie dust.

"Come for a tumble, love?"

The Woodcutter closed the door behind him.

The tainted magic, cut with charms to stretch the product for maximum profit, stung his eyes.

"Your daughter is dead," he said.

The woman blinked.

And then she sighed and reached across the table to do another line of pixie dust.

He waited as she let the magic slide from her nostrils down the back of her throat.

"Little bitch had it coming."

Blonde curls against the wooden floor.

He sat down in a chair. The free magic was making him dizzy.

He willed his lips to move. "Do you have any enemies?"

She looked at him incredulously. "She was probably killed by one of those wolf things that's always going around eating up children."

A true mother would never have sent her daughter into the Wood dressed in a red cape.

The flowers scattered...

He looked down at his folded hands. "She did not have a mark upon her. Neither she nor your mother."

The woman sat up, suddenly alert. "My mother? What happened to my mother?"

She read it in his eyes before he was able to say the words.

She began screaming.

Screaming that he was a liar. Screaming that it wasn't true.

Screaming.

And screaming.

And screaming.

The Madam rushed into the room and held the woman tight to her bosom, rocking her gently and forcing a vial of liquid to her lips.

The screams slowed and then stopped, and the woman fell into sleep.

The Madam looked at the woman and then at the Woodcutter. "If you hurt a hair—"

"Her child and her mother were found dead just a few hours ago."

The Madam stroked the whore's head and sighed. "She won't be much use to me for a while."

She fell silent, her cold words hanging in the air.

"Did she have any enemies?" asked the Woodcutter.

"None that I know," the Madam shrugged.

"The dust trade?"

"She used. Never dealt."

"Any other girls gone missing lately?"

The Madam shook her head, then she stopped herself. "Wait. Not one of mine, but some servant a few nights back—whatever the night the Prince had that ball. Stella. Ella. Something. She might have shown back up, but her stepmother was looking for her."

The Woodcutter rose and flicked a wooden coin at her. The Madam caught it in her palm.

"Let me know if you see her."

CHAPTER 10

He stared at the ceiling, awake in his spartan room at the empty inn. Midnight had come and gone. The bed's straw tick poked at his skin. He tossed off the blankets and walked to the window, opening it to the night air.

The one body had become three: a woman in glass slippers, dressed in a ball gown of white, a grandmother sleeping in her bed, and the half-fae child with golden hair. All three killed without a mark, but all three covered in the same stench of fear.

He looked at the moon and could almost feel his wife's soft hair against his skin, the way she fit perfectly between his jaw and his shoulder. There had been that day so many years ago... that day when she had first rested her head against him, when everything was still new and tentative. They had watched the sun go down and waited to count the stars in the sky, speaking of everything and nothing.

I shall look at the moon and wait for you, my love...

Three chances before he would have to visit the River God again.

He lay back down and closed his eyes.

CHAPTER 11

The village disappeared beneath the horizon as he made his way to the Wood. The trees swayed in greeting; they knew him here.

The Woodcutter inhaled deeply, searching for the tainted scent he first smelled on the woman with glass slippers. The wind brought him no answers. He slowed his pace, looking at the vegetation for bruises or broken branches. He searched the ground, looking everywhere for a sign.

The boot impression was almost hidden in the dry dirt and pine needles. The next footprint was small and delicate, slightly larger than the palm of his hand. Deeper and deeper into the Wood he followed the tracks left unwittingly by their owners.

A flash of dark hair between the branches and leaves caught the corner of his eye. He crept forward.

A young girl cried softly.

Hair as black as ebony.

He relaxed and allowed the leaves to crunch beneath his feet.

Skin as white as snow.

She leapt up.

Lips as red as blood.

As blood.

Blood.

And that was when he realized things were horribly wrong.

In her hand was a dagger. Lying at her feet was the body of a huntsman. And upon her snow-white skin was the dark-red stain of blood.

She cried out hysterically, "Do not come a step closer!"

The huntsman. Slashed across the neck. Stabbed in the heart. Fresh crimson poured from his still-warm body.

The Woodcutter held out his hands as a sign of peace to the terrified princess.

"I know you! I know you, Huntsman! Come to cut out my heart and deliver it in a box to the Queen," she screamed.

He saw the glamour on the blade.

He softened his voice. "I am but a humble woodcutter, not a huntsman."

Her trembling hand lowered a fraction of an inch.

"I was drawn by your cries," he said.

She wiped away a tear, leaving a streak of red across her cheek.

"I mean you no harm."

She gulped. Then hiccupped.

"You seem to have some trouble here."

Her voice wavered. "He tried to kill me."

The Woodcutter nodded as he glanced over her body from head to toe. She was marked purple and blue by bruises and scrapes. Huntsmen were supposed to be moved by pity to leave young girls untouched in the Wood. Her innocence lost, she would no longer be able to converse with the animals that would have protected her.

The Queen's power was growing. The story was being changed— the girl in the glass shoes, the Small One with the red cape, now the Princess of the Sixth Kingdom herself.

The trees seemed to cry.

"Come with me," the Woodcutter murmured.

She raised the knife in panic.

He continued to hold out his hands, speaking to her gently. "The blade you hold has been spelled."

She seemed to be listening, but he could see her pulse pounding in her throat.

"It will turn your hand against yourself if it does not cause death again soon. If you put it on the ground, I can help you. There is a cottage nearby that I can take you to, a cottage where you will be safe..."

His voice repeated the instructions over and over. He allowed just a little bit of magic to whisper into the words. Snow White's lids began to drift closed. Her fingers relaxed and the blade slipped.

He had her in his arms before she could fall.

As the knife sped toward the earth, it spun and impaled itself hilt first into the ground. Its bewitched blade stared up at him hungrily, like a baby bird begging for food.

"You are a nasty one," he said to the knife.

He knew it was not his imagination that a shadow winked back at him along the metal's sharp edge.

He carried the Princess to the safety of a tree and leaned her against its strong trunk. The tree shifted its branches to cradle her reclining form.

The Woodcutter unsheathed the Silver Ax and walked toward the knife.

The energy seemed to sizzle as the two objects sized each other up. He felt the Ax tremble in his hand with excitement, a guard dog being held back from attack.

He swung the Ax above his head and struck the tip of the knife true.

A thunderclap sounded as storm clouds darkened the sky.

He gritted his teeth as the Ax powered its way through. He heard the knife scream. Its wild magic was no match for the elemental powers contained in the Ax.

The wind whipped around him.

The Ax continued its work, cutting through the knife from point to hilt, fueled only by the authority of the Woodcutter.

A lightning bolt struck the Ax, and the knife disappeared in its flash of blinding white light. The Ax dissolved into water.

But the storm did not break as it should have. Instead, the wind cried, *RUN!*

The Woodcutter threw Snow White over his shoulder and raced into the day as dark as night.

The Beast raised his nose.

His blind eyes shone silver in the darkness.

He chuffed the cold air, coating his mouth with the taste of the wild, untamed magic calling him to the hunt.

He howled at the trees, howled at them as they screamed warning to his prey.

The Woodcutter stopped. He did not breathe. He covered the Princess's mouth with his hand. The trees whispered, *Quietly! Quietly!* as they lowered their branches to hide him.

A wind roared past, and he knew it held the creature he sought.

But he waited. He waited with the Princess until the night lifted and the day returned to its proper hour. He waited until the voices of the trees returned to their gentle sigh.

Then he gathered up the Princess in his arms, leaning her head against his shoulder, and continued walking.

CHAPTER 12

The door to the cottage was open. The small body of a tiny man lay over the threshold. His hand still clasped the handle, although he no longer breathed.

The Woodcutter wearily placed the Princess down.

The body was followed by six more throughout the cottage, each in a position of flight, each dead without a mark.

The Woodcutter returned to the front door and leaned his hand against it. It was a door made of solid oak. The life of the tree should have warded the home against evil, if only the men had been able to make it inside.

The door to the Grandmother's house was ajar...

He did not understand this force that had been summoned by the bewitched knife, this thing that killed without a mark, this creature that did not have to wait for the sun to go down to strike.

He carried the Princess and laid her across the seven small beds. He knew that this was the appointed place for the Princess to hide. If it was no longer safe, then the force they faced was beyond his powers.

He then carried the seven bodies out into the yard and buried them, not willing to risk the magic necessary to give them the traditional rites of pyre and light. He could sense that their spirits had already left. They were not clinging to their bodies. He could feel it. It was strange that the knowledge brought him no peace.

He sighed and ran his fingers through his beard.

He would stay.

If the creature returned, he would protect the Princess.

And he did not want to risk the coming night alone.

CHAPTER 13

The Princess's eyes fluttered open. They seemed to focus upon the seven headboards. She sat up, taking in the room and its diminutive furniture.

She turned to the Woodcutter. The crusted blood cracked on her face and lazy flakes dusted the sheets.

"Do little children live here?"

The Woodcutter looked at the young woman. Not yet seventeen. Sixteen and at the prime of magic's peak. Her heart would have been a dear treasure for the Queen.

"There are no children here," he said. The Woodcutter could not help the deadly chill that ran through his bones. "No one lives here anymore."

She looked at him. She had more intelligence in her eyes than most princesses he had met.

"There were supposed to be people living here...weren't there...?"

The question trailed off.

But it remained in her eyes.

Those intelligent eyes.

Blue eyes against the blonde curls.

His mind retched at the thought of the tiny hands gathering flowers just yesterday, of the small hands of the men he had just buried.

The Princess looked down at the burgundy stains upon her white skin.

"There was supposed to be someone here," she whispered.

She began trying to rub off the blood, dabbing her fingertips to her tongue and furiously wiping the red upon her arms. "This should never have been on my skin," she said.

The Woodcutter took her hands in his and held them upon her lap until they stilled.

She looked at him. Her eyes were brown, not blue.

Blue eyes open beneath the blonde curls.

Her eyes were brown against her black hair. Large tears welled in those eyes, spilling over and creating paths in the blood. "I do not understand…"

He held her hands quiet and allowed her to cry.

He did not understand, either.

CHAPTER 14

His wife was far better at comfort, he thought, as he poured the boiling water into the small cup.

The Princess held her knees to her chest, wrapped up in a blanket as if it could shield her from what she had seen and done.

She had washed away the stains from earlier and her clothes soaked in a tub nearby.

"Thank you," she said, taking the cup from the Woodcutter.

He grunted in acknowledgment.

"Who are you?" she asked.

"I am the Woodcutter," he replied simply.

"So you cut wood?"

"No."

"Then how can you be a woodcutter?"

"I am the Woodcutter."

"I do not know what that means."

She should have, he thought. She should have known the name *Woodcutter*, for his father and his father's father had overseen the crowning of every heir in the Sixth Kingdom for the past one hundred years. He knew her. He had brought her gifts from the fae days after her birth. Indeed, it was he that brought skin of snow and hair of ebony and lips as red as mortal blood.

She should have been told stories of him upon her father's knee. Her father should have told her of the treaty between the fae and humans and of the Woodcutter who held the peace. More importantly, she should have been warned why she, as royalty, as a blue-blooded half-fae, should never venture into the Woodcutter's forest until her heart had discovered true love.

Instead, her ignorance had led her to spill blood at the base of his trees. Blood bound one to the forest, and the water soaking her clothes was dark red.

He stood and poured the water out from the wash bin, refilling it from a pump carved to look like fish there in the kitchen.

Blood bound blood, and she was bound.

"Why were you in the Wood, Princess?" he asked.

She wrapped the blanket more tightly. "I do not know."

She was lying. And he knew it. He sat down in front of her and quietly waited.

The words were soft and hesitant when they finally flowed from her lips. "I woke this morning and went to the garden...It was as if the sun had forgotten to rise. The sky was dark and not a creature stirred. There is a pond in my garden with a weeping willow beside it. It has always been my haven. But instead of my pond, I found a mansion I had never seen before. It was as if faeries had come and built it overnight.

"Its door stood open. I called for the owner, but no one replied. I entered, which was foolish, but I only hoped to find the answer to the mystery. The rooms were strange. One would look like it was morning and the one beside it would be as dark as night. But then I came to a wooden door, which opened into some sort of workroom. There was a spiral staircase going down. I followed those stairs and at the bottom..."

She paused, as if gathering her strength to survive the memory.

"I found a prison. The walls were lined with iron cages, and inside, they were filled with pixies—thousands of pixies. They were dying. I tried to free as many as I could, but they were so many and they were so weak..."

She looked at the Woodcutter. She looked at him with haunted eyes that pleaded to forget the memory. "Have you ever heard a pixie touch the earth?"

He had.

He had seen and heard many things a person should never see or hear in their lifetime.

He reached out and gripped her hand, grimly.

"Their magic was being siphoned off," she said. "Bottles and bottles of dust lined the walls...fresh, wild magic. They had been bled dry. I freed as many as I could..." There was a note of frustration in her voice. "As many as I could..."

He wanted to touch her shoulder reassuringly.

But he didn't.

Instead, he poured her more tea.

She stared into the depths of the liquid. "I knew I needed to get them to the Wood."

The Woodcutter's eyebrows raised in surprise before his face disappeared once more into a mask of control. He was surprised, for all her ignorance, she knew this. Once bound by iron, the life of wood could best reverse the effects upon the fae.

"I placed them in a basket and brought them here, but as I entered the Wood, the Huntsman saw me. He had been following me, I am sure. I ran to the clearing and tried to give the pixies to the trees. But the Huntsman started killing them. He killed so many. They were just lying on the ground...They tried to protect me...All I wanted to do was to save them...He just kept slicing and stabbing with that knife and their light kept getting dimmer...the sound as each one touched the earth...He wouldn't stop, even though I begged him...He wouldn't stop..."

Her eyes bore deep into the Woodcutter's.

"So I killed him."

The Woodcutter rose to his feet.

The fae were as close to immortal as any creature could be. That the knife had been able to kill them...that this Huntsman carried a tool that could kill a faerie...and that this princess was strong enough to wield the knife to kill the Huntsman...

"Stay here," he said.

CHAPTER 15

Two hours until nightfall.

He stood in the clearing.

The trees were silent, mute in shock and horror.

The pixies were splayed in unnatural positions, their blue blood pooled upon the ground.

Revenge.

The word burned in his mind, burned in anger, burned with a hatred that blinded him. The trees softly murmured their command: *Revenge.*

His fingers felt along the handle of his Golden Ax as he looked at the Huntsman's corpse. He reached out with his senses, letting his mind drift with the wind over the blades of grass and into the smallest crevices of every rock and tree. The Huntsman's spirit still wandered nearby, waiting by its body until midnight, when the door to the afterlife would open.

It would do.

The Woodcutter opened his eyes, and his sight fell upon an ancient elm, a tree whose voice had called out the loudest.

He walked over and placed his hands upon the elm's trunk. He could feel the sap flowing, feel the life within the wood. He asked the dark-green tree for a sacrifice, to taint its existence for revenge, and the elm replied without hesitation, *Yes.*

Just then, the Woodcutter's ears caught a whisper.

Hope, the trees whispered, first one and then a chorus.

Hope, their leaves shivered as they stretched their branches out to point at the fallen fae.

The Woodcutter looked upon the ground.

His eyes caught the faintest flicker of light, and he sprinted to its side.

It was alive. One small pixie was still alive.

He gently picked it up. It was so tiny it fit in his cupped hands. It was pale blue with such black eyes. It did not weigh as much as a feather.

Its light kept flashing in and out as it gasped for breath.

He hurried to the closest tree, an oak that had lowered a limb to take the tiny one.

He placed the pixie in the bough, and the tree whispered, *Yes.*

He would never cut unless invited, unless absolutely necessary. But the tree had whispered *yes* and so he did.

He removed the Golden Ax from his side and sliced down the middle of the branch. The Ax cut the bark like a hot knife through butter.

He felt the tree shiver in pain.

The sap ran dark as the wound deepened, as the tree pulled itself apart to widen the incision.

The Woodcutter transferred the dying pixie into the wound.

He felt the pixie and the tree sigh at the contact.

He held the Ax above the cut as it dissolved into water—clean, purifying water to wash away the evil.

The pixie raised its head, drinking in the gift of the River God.

The Woodcutter caught a sleepy smile as the wound sealed the pixie within the tree, to be fed and nurtured until the next spring, when the pixie would be reborn within the first flowering of the first blossom, healed and whole once again.

He rested his hand against the tree in thanks for the sacrifice and the gift.

Two Axes gone.

CHAPTER 16

The Woodcutter placed the small forget-me-nots upon the hearts of the remaining pixies.

He stepped away and a swaying shadow fell across his face, the swaying shadow of the dead Huntsman, now hanging by his neck from the dark-green elm.

The Woodcutter checked the knot holding the noose.

The bodies of the fae circled the Huntsman's feet, binding him to walk the earth. They kept his soul from rest. He would be bound until one could be called to deal with him as was fit.

The Woodcutter looked down at his pack, fingering the pocket that held the black bag.

He did not need to do this, he told himself.

The trees whispered, *Revenge.*

He looked at the pixies, their tiny shapes lying so still upon the ground. They should never have touched the earth.

Such small hands.

Small hands.

Blonde curls.

A little leg turned at a wrong angle.

Flowers on the floor.

He pushed away the memory.

Sunset was fading, and the Woodcutter shivered.

He settled himself at the base of the tree and lit his pipe, waiting for midnight to come.

CHAPTER 17

The Woodcutter jerked awake, disoriented at first. The hanging Huntsman reminded him where he was. He looked up at the sky, at the full moon on the rise. It was almost midnight. He had not slept too long.

He stood, and the trees around him slowly stirred as his hand moved toward the bag. He felt them form a sleepy barrier, knowing what was to come. He heard their leaves whisper the spells. His hand grasped the black bag, and the whole forest seemed to hold its breath.

He opened the bag and shivered as a current of raw power surged up his arm. His fingers wrapped around the humble instrument inside and lifted the horn to his lips.

And he blew.

The sound that emerged was a hurricane. The trees bent. The wind whipped. The air tasted of fresh rain. The sound reverberated across the Wood, across the Twelve Kingdoms, across the Land.

Dark clouds rolled across the moon and pitched him into the blackest of night.

The trees screamed out warning to any that might hear: *Stay to the middle of the path! The Hunt rides!*

The Woodcutter lowered the horn and waited.

The baying of dogs echoed across the clearing, echoed as they came down from the sky.

He closed his eyes, willing away the urge to run, to run to the end of the earth and farther beyond, to do anything but to face the coming dogs.

Their snarls and growls drew closer. Closer.

Then he heard the hooves of the Raging Host, of their carnivorous horses trampling the ground. The beasts were ridden by the souls powerful enough to control them—a horde of male warriors chosen to ride the night sky instead of surrendering to the caresses of eternal sleep, a pack of bare-breasted Valkyrie women who intoxicatingly called people to their doom, a band of the dead who lusted for nothing but the Hunt.

He felt hot breath upon his cheek. He heard the metal jangle against the warm leather.

He opened his eyes.

Before him stood the eight-legged horse, Sleipnir. The eight-legged horse sired by Svadifari and out of Loki.

And upon him sat the Rider.

The Master of the Hunt.

The King of Valhalla.

Odin.

The god's hawkish eye stared golden and unblinking through the slit in his horned helmet. His hellhounds milled like moonlit fog at his feet, their shadow teeth brushed against the Woodcutter, waiting only for Odin's command to rip and tear into such sweet-smelling flesh.

The Woodcutter bowed in respect, but was careful not to bow in subservience.

The Rider tilted his head. "Woodcutter."

"Odin."

Their names were charged with magic. It crackled the air about them and caused the Valkyries' mounts to dance.

Odin eyed the hanging body of the Huntsman. "A sacrifice."

The observation was tinged with pleasure. Odin pointed his finger and the hellhounds stalked toward the corpse. But then they stopped, unable to pass beyond the ring of fallen fae. One turned and whimpered to his master. Odin pulled on Sleipnir's reins and drew close. He looked down upon the circle of pixie corpses.

The clouds began to rumble.

"Who would commit such an atrocity?" he roared as Sleipnir reared up against the night.

As the wind tore the words from his throat, the Woodcutter extended his arm and shouted, "Him that hangs from the branch. I have bound him to this earth for anyone who can mete out proper justice."

The world became very still as Odin looked down upon the Woodcutter. "You are sly, my friend."

And then Odin began to laugh. He laughed a terrible, horrible laugh that splintered the sky. "Indeed, someday I shall hunt you, but tonight, your revenge shall feed the Wild Hunt."

Odin barked a guttural command, and the hellhounds' noses shot to the ground. He turned back to the Woodcutter, his voice full of menace. "And now I name the price. There are those that meddle within my realms. One of my very own hounds refuses to answer my call."

A cold grain of fear burned in the Woodcutter's belly.

"Return to me my hound."

It was a command, not a request. The Woodcutter bowed his head, feeling the weight of a million worlds placed like a yoke upon his shoulders.

"Do not look so down," Odin laughed. "Afterward, if you wish to Hunt, you can join the Ride."

A mournful howl rose from the throat of a hellhound.

Sleipnir snorted fire from his nose.

"We Hunt!" Odin commanded.

The mounts screamed and the hellhounds cried as the wild magic broke like a wave upon the shore, led by Odin into the night.

A single Valkyrie grabbed the Huntsman's corpse. She swung the body in circles above her head by the tail of the hangman's noose as she disappeared between the trees.

CHAPTER 18

The Woodcutter watched as the Hunt's noises faded into the chaos of the storm, a storm that would rage until dawn.

He looked around the clearing. The grass had not been touched by the hooves of the Wild Hunt's beasts.

The circle of the fae seemed so small and sad now that their purpose was done.

He turned.

Snow White stood silhouetted in the moon. Her eyes held the wildness reserved for beasts. They were eyes that had seen too much.

She had seen the Hunt.

And she had not run.

The Woodcutter knew the price she must have paid to still her legs and will them to hold their ground.

"Princess…" he said as he stepped toward her.

She shook her head as her blue blood, blood thick with ancestry of fae, claimed a mind that no longer wished to be human.

"Princess…"

Like a hind, she stood ready to fly. Like a creature of the Wood, she dared him to follow.

"Princess…" And he waved his hand, quietly striking her with his spell.

She slumped to the ground.

He was suddenly tired.

Very, very tired.

But the night was not over, for at that moment his ears picked up the most peculiar sound—a million tiny bells, pinpricks of gladness within the wild night.

The wind stopped abruptly, although the trees outside the clearing still swayed.

All exhaustion left him.

He reached a hand to the tree beside him to keep the glamour from his eyes. He could feel its sap beat in time with his heart. He breathed in, trying to force his mind to remember that which was drawing close.

The bells awakened a memory from a lifetime ago.

A memory of being at his father's side.

Honeysuckle.

Night-blooming jasmine.

He breathed out and welcomed the soft purple light as two small creatures flew into the meadow and then another two.

Faeries filled the clearing, their radiance chasing away the darkness. A happiness settled into his heart as the trees whispered glad greetings.

And then his heart seemed to stop.

It was a sight not meant for human eyes, but he had seen it once before.

On a litter, supported by four cloven-hoofed fauns, rode an impossibly beautiful couple with skin so pale it seemed to capture light and reflect it. Flowers bloomed at their feet in a never-ending cycle of birth and fell from the litter, leaving a trail of life wherever the couple was carried.

The Woodcutter fell to his knees, his hand still pressed against the tree.

The fauns lowered the litter to the ground and the couple rose. Their slender limbs seemed to glide.

"Your Highnesses," the Woodcutter whispered.

Queen Titania smiled gently at him before touching her husband's sleeve. "Oberon, we have found here our greatest friend."

The glamour was almost too strong, the ecstasy of being in their presence too much.

Only one finger remained on the tree.

Only one finger guarded him from madness.

Oberon looked at the tiny bodies of the murdered pixies. His face held such infinite sadness. He walked to their circle and waved his long fingers over their forms. "Sleep, my young ones. No longer children of air, I give you to the earth."

Quietly, the earth cradled their bodies, and quietly, the earth covered them in a blanket of dirt as soft as an embrace. Soon there was nothing but a barren ring of freshly turned dirt.

"Until we meet again," he said.

Oberon walked to the hangman's tree and touched the elm's sturdy trunk. "Gentle friend, we thank you for your sacrifice. By my touch, I remove the deed from your sap and once again you grow untainted."

The tree seemed to lean into King Oberon's hand, seemed to almost sigh.

But then Queen Titania raised her chin, listening to a gentle whisper. "But there is reason to celebrate," she said. She walked to the outstretched limb of one of the trees and ran her hand across the fresh cut that covered the injured pixie. "Gentle friend, within you rests one who otherwise would have died."

A million lights danced in the night.

She lowered her lips and laid a silver kiss upon the wound. "In the spring, indeed you shall blossom, and in the spring, such life you will bring forth. You will live for many ages, and your kindness will not be forgotten by my people. Gentle rains shall wash you, and gentle winds shall be your friend. Forever will this grove be protected—forever, because of your love."

She passed her hand once more across the cut, and where it passed, the bark was restored.

Then she stopped, staring at the fallen Princess Snow White, who lay in silent slumber.

The Queen raised her hands and a host of her handmaidens flew to the girl. Titania looked fondly upon Snow White and whispered tenderly, "Good Princess, gentle soul of mortal and faerie, we are bound by the blood of the Huntsman to bind you to our realm for eternity. But because your deed was committed in defense of our most beloved, you shall be our honored guest and shall be protected by us, your shared people, until the need is no more."

Queen Titania's ladies came forward and surrounded Snow White in glowing light. Slowly her body lifted from the ground, lifted up on ribbons of color and air.

King Oberon returned to the litter and held his hand out for his wife to join him. She ascended, her movements like a summer's doe. King Oberon turned to the Woodcutter as the litter was raised. "We thank you for honoring our fallen brethren. We have heard the Wild Hunt and know that justice will be done."

King Oberon observed the sky. "Too much magic has been taken. The veil between the mortal and immortal is crossed by one whose foot should never pass. We have learned that Odin's hound runs free. Seek out the Crone for the answers. We shall meet when the Hunt rides again."

Queen Titania raised her palm in blessing. "Like your father before you and his father before that, these Woods shall be your friend for as long as you remain our servant. We shall be your people until beyond the time your soul outgrows such mortal trappings. Terrible dangers walk the night, and to you alone falls the task of setting these Woods right."

The Woodcutter reached out in thanks.

And his last finger left the safety of the tree.

His eyes closed, overwhelmed by the glamour.

A million bells rang sweetly in his ears.

A million feather touches passed over his skin.

A million quiet voices whispered and giggled.

Seek out the Crone...

Seek out the Crone...

His eyes opened to the dawn. A perfect ring of forget-me-nots grew in wild profusion beneath the gentle shadows of a dark-green elm tree.

CHAPTER 19

He strapped the Platinum Ax to one side and his father's ax to the other. He had one more chance before he would have to return to the River God and risk a trial that could lose his father's ax forever.

Seek out the Crone.

He turned his head in the wind and closed his eyes.

A soft breeze blew across his cheek.

He stretched his senses to the earth, and a golden glow seemed to come just off to the left of where he was standing.

He opened his eyes, settled his pack more comfortably upon his shoulders, and began his journey.

CHAPTER 20

The mansion was new.

Sometimes the landscape would shift to confuse weary travelers and those who should not wander in the Wood, but the Woodcutter could feel the true paths. He knew this one, and the mansion had not been there before.

It rose five stories, with slender white pillars supporting a darkly gabled roof. Surrounding it was a carefully tamed garden, its pruned bushes and manicured lawn sharply contrasting against the wildness of the Wood, the property line divided betwixt the two by a curled-iron fence.

It must be dealt with. The Woodcutter loosened the Platinum Ax. The Wood did strange things to humans, especially humans who had a distant touch of the fae within. It turned them from ordinary people into mad hermits, cannibals who ate children thinking they were made of gingerbread, and people who swore they had been asleep for one hundred years.

If a person's blood ran royal blue and his magic was powerful enough, one might survive the Wood. To live, it was either full magic or none at all.

Or none at all…

None at all…

His wife.

His hands rested upon the gate to the mansion, and he could almost feel her plain fingers upon his shoulder.

Her caring, ordinary touch as she brought him his pipe as he sat by the fire at night… as she brought him a steaming cup of coffee in the morning for no other reason than to tell him that she loved him, for no other reason than to express in an ordinary way that she cared…

A cup of steaming coffee…

The steam from the tea he had set before the Princess…

The water in the basin, red with the blood of the Huntsman…

He forced the memory away.

He opened the gate and stepped onto the grounds. A low mist appeared, swirling around his legs as if tasting him. He kicked it away and walked to the imposing house.

He knocked upon the door, and when no answer was forthcoming, he knocked again. The door swung open silently.

He stepped into the entry, tiled in gray-and-white marble. The windows were swathed in heavy black drapes. Odd music trickled down the hall, echoing empty, hollow notes. He walked toward the music and found himself before a large double door that stood ajar.

Inside was a ballroom with lit candles that flickered dim in the gray light of day. The room was filled with snoring bodies of lords and ladies reclining upon mutely colored couches. They were sleeping, yet dressed in evening splendor. Feathered heads and powdered wigs leaned against jewel-bedecked bosoms and tilted shoulders.

But one person was awake—a frighteningly pale gentleman with bloodred lips and dark circles under his eyes. He sat at a piano, playing the drifting tune that called the Woodcutter.

The Gentleman looked up as the Woodcutter picked his way through the room. His words lolled out casually, "Come to sample the dust? Or merely to be a part of such lively company?"

Even relaxed, the Gentleman moved like a panther in the jungle. The Woodcutter's hand never left the Platinum Ax.

"How did this House come to be in my Wood?" asked the Woodcutter.

The Gentleman banged out a doomful arpeggio in mock horror. "Your Wood? My, I had no idea."

"How did you come to my Wood?" the Woodcutter asked again.

"Well, it is a funny thing. We went to sleep one night, woke the next morrow, and here we were." The Gentleman let out a childlike giggle and waved a lace-trimmed hand at the resting bodies. "So, you see, we decided to make the best of things, and may I just say we are having a simply splendid time. Hope you don't mind, these being your Woods and all…What did you say your name was?"

The Woodcutter felt the tendril of magic quietly try to sneak up on him.

There was power behind it.

"Those that need to know my name, do," said the Woodcutter.

The Gentleman stopped playing and rested his arms upon the piano. "But I need to know. I absolutely must know your name." He began a wandering trill. "For how else will I know to whom to engrave the invitation, since it seems you have entered my House uninvited."

There was a dangerous gleam in the Gentleman's eye.

The Woodcutter bowed. "I shall take my leave. Please move your home. You are not welcome here."

The Gentleman leapt to his feet. "No! Stay. What sort of a host do you take me to be? Where are my manners? Of course we're not welcome in your Wood. I have been acting like an absolute bore. Here, let me introduce you to the rest of the guests. Do help yourself to the dust. We have loads."

He clapped his hands, and sparkling embers fell from the ceiling.

Faerie dust.

The Woodcutter held his breath and covered his head with his jacket, but the dust was too thick. He felt it on his skin, seeping into his bloodstream. It felt like slipping into a warm spring and waking in a dream.

There was a flash and the room was at once alive, awash in reds and golds and filled with joyous revelers. It was dark outside, but the party was bright beneath the blazing candelabras.

The Woodcutter spun, unsteady on his feet and caught in the middle of the dance floor as lords and ladies glided by. The violins played. Laughter swept by.

He did not know where he was or how he had gotten there.

The Woodcutter looked over at the musicians' stage and at a Gentleman performing upon the piano.

The Gentleman gave the Woodcutter a wink.

The Woodcutter thought he might have met the Gentleman before. He took a step toward the dais, but the world seemed to tilt. The Woodcutter staggered and was caught as a tightly laced bodice pressed up against his side.

"Are you feeling quite well?"

He nodded his head and gratefully patted the arm that held him. His tongue was thick and could not move properly. The lady helped him regain his balance and then said, "I do not believe we have been properly introduced."

The lady wore scarlet brocade and held out a gloved hand. Her hair was so black it was blue, and her skin was painted white. She smelled of spice and forbidden thoughts. Her pulse beat its rhythm in the delicate dip between her throat and her collarbone. A small beauty patch shaped like a flower sat upon her cheek.

He could not keep his eyes off the beauty patch.

She placed her hand in his. "Monsieur...?"

She stared at him expectantly.

But he said nothing, for he could not remember.

Her dark eyes flashed as she clapped her hands. "A game, is it? Let me see if I can guess…"

He pushed past, his mind upon the beauty patch.

A flower.

Something…

Something about flowers…

The woman's hand rested once again upon his arm. "Sir…"

He turned.

She leaned against him.

"Who are you?" she whispered. Her lips were so close to his ear. She held her finger to her red mouth playfully. "Our secret. I shall not tell another soul. Just tell me your name."

The Woodcutter peeled himself away, asking, "How does a person leave this place?"

She pointed to a door across the ballroom. "That way, but you should not leave now," she pouted.

"Why?" he asked.

"Because you will miss all the fun."

He walked toward the door, uncertain of anything except that he should not be at this ball.

"Prince baiting," the woman in red called.

He stopped and turned. "What?"

She walked slowly toward him, her eyes never leaving his. "Prince baiting. We seem to have caught one mid-quest. If he wins, he goes free. Of course, they never win."

She leaned against the Woodcutter and pointed at a servant standing near a pillar. He was a tall man with a strong chin. He glowered at the crowd as he held the tray of snuffboxes.

"Mr. Charming was quite a fighter," she said.

"Are there others?" asked the Woodcutter. He did not know why the question was important, but something inside told him it was so.

The woman waved her fingers at the other servants. The Woodcutter counted six men in all.

"Here the royalty wait upon us," she purred, stepping away. "Oh, dear"—she smiled at him like a cat with a bird in its mouth— "I forgot to mention it before. I am afraid the prince we shall be baiting tonight is you."

The Woodcutter turned.

The revelers had surrounded him, their merriment transformed to menace. The Woodcutter felt strong hands upon his arms, holding him tightly from behind. He struggled to pull away, but the grips only strengthened.

The Gentleman entered the ring, tucking a handkerchief back into his sleeve. He held his hand out to the woman in red. "My Queen."

She drew close and placed a lingering kiss upon his cheek.

As she stepped into the crowd, the guests parted and dropped low on bent knee before her.

"Well," said the Gentleman to the Woodcutter, "I suppose you will want to know the rules. Win, you go free. Lose, you stay here and serve me. At your ready."

The Woodcutter was silent and then shook his head.

The Gentleman laughed. "Oh, my dear prince, I'm afraid you don't get a say in this." Then he looked at the Woodcutter from the corner of his eye and tutted. "Isn't it unfair…?"

The Woodcutter still had not moved. His gaze was upon the six imprisoned princes who stood voiceless and impassive, carrying the silver trays loaded with dust boxes. Finally he spoke. "I want higher stakes."

This made the Gentleman stop. "Higher stakes? I do believe this is a first! What fun!" The Gentleman circled like a tiger. "Very well. If I win, you become mine and these Woods become my permanent domain."

The Woodcutter fingered the shiny Ax that hung at his side. He did not know the woods to which the Gentleman was referring, but he knew he opposed anything the man wanted. He nodded. "If I win, you leave the woods and you free the princes whom you hold prisoner," said the Woodcutter.

"Good! We have a deal," said the Gentleman. The crowd clapped appreciatively. "And now to the game."

A table was brought forward, a table bearing a knife.

There was a darkness to the knife, something about it that burned the Woodcutter's nose.

"Pick it up," said the Gentleman.

The Woodcutter found the knife in his hands.

"Here is the game. You will begin cutting yourself."

The Woodcutter saw the knife move to his arm, moved by his own hand but not by a will of his own.

He fought.

He fought hard.

Yet he felt the jagged-toothed edge cold against his skin.

"You will sit here and cut yourself until you tell me your name. And then I win. Or you don't tell me your name and you'll win, but you'll die." The Gentleman giggled to the crowd, delighted by his own deviousness. "And I promise, afterward, I shall set you free."

And then the Woodcutter felt the serrations rip into his flesh.

The pain was blinding as the knife grazed against his bone.

The Gentleman smiled as he sat and took a glass of wine from a passing prince's tray. "Such a fun game."

A man shouted across the circle, "I say he doesn't last ten cuts."

The Gentleman shouted back, "I have a box of dust that says he only lasts five."

The Woodcutter felt the knife line up for another cut. He tried to will his hand to still.

The pain was enormous. White light flashed before his eyes. Black replaced it as dots swam before him.

But he remembered.

He remembered his name. He remembered his name and that he must protect himself. He felt his blood gushing out, sticky and warm down his arms and his legs and into his shoes.

The knife still cut on.

"All you have to do to get it all to stop is just whisper your name," said the Gentleman.

The request rippled through the undulating crowd.

"Your name…"

"Your name…"

And then a faint whisper, "His blood runs red."

A louder whisper spat, "Silence."

It took all his energy to not let them see it ran a different color.

"Your name…"

The call taunted him.

"Just say your name…"

So easy, he thought.

Just his name…

He looked up and saw the leering face of the beautiful woman in scarlet. His blood had splattered across her cheek, across her beauty patch. She looked at the Woodcutter and slowly licked a droplet off her upper lip.

The beauty patch.

The flower.

Flowers.

Flowers scattered upon the floor.

A small hand.

Golden curls…

Chestnut hair.

And a plain face with a welcome smile that had greeted him for ten years and ten years more…

His wife.

"Never."

And the Woodcutter took the dagger and plunged it into his own heart.

Suddenly the room was gone.

The Woodcutter was standing in the gray room with the revelers still fast asleep around him.

The Gentleman downed a quick cordial. "Oh, bother. What a way to end a perfectly good game," he said.

The Woodcutter said nothing.

"Well, I suppose you will want me to move my house, Prince of the Wood," the Gentleman laughed, trying to lighten the mood.

But the Woodcutter remained silent. His arms still felt the pain of the phantom cuts; his chest still felt the knife as it entered.

The Gentleman's face flashed frustration. "You are a terrible sport. Look, no one was hurt. Just a bit of fun. I don't know why you have to be—"

In two steps, the Woodcutter was at the fop's side. His closed fist connected with the Gentleman's jaw and struck him to the ground.

"Get out of my Wood," he rumbled.

The Gentleman picked himself up, blue blood pouring from his nose. He hissed at the Woodcutter, "Oh, you shall pay. You shall have your princes, but not here. Go find them, dog."

And with that, the mansion disappeared and the Woodcutter found himself standing alone in the forest.

CHAPTER 21

Prince of the Wood.

The Woodcutter looked at the place the mansion, the Vanishing House, had once stood.

The Gentleman had wanted the Wood.

There had been someone else there, too. The Woodcutter searched his mind, but the memory of her was fading. All he could remember was scarlet red and a hand upon his arm, but then even that was gone.

The face of the Gentleman remained.

It took a mighty magic to construct such a home...and the dust. So much pixie dust...

The powdered magic had always been a problem. To humans, it was irresistible. The Woodcutter rubbed his forehead, still unbalanced. He and the fae were creatures of the natural elements—wind and fire, earth and water. But when faerie magic was stolen, it became wild, and the chaos of siphoned pixie dust clashed with the order of his way.

One hundred centuries ago, twelve tribes of humans first tasted the wild power of faerie magic and hungered to make it their own. A terrible battle between the two worlds occurred. Mankind did not win.

And so the Twelve Kingdoms were established. The fae knew that humans were creatures of both the light and the dark, existing in careful balance between the two forces. They decreed that as long as half the Twelve Kingdoms swore to live peacefully, the fae would not annihilate the race of man.

Twelve faerie rulers were placed upon those twelve thrones. It was sworn that the blood of the Kingdoms' rulers must always run blue.

But a remarkable discovery was made.

Love.

The Faerie King Stephan, harsh and cold, had looked upon the crowd as he rode through the Seventh Kingdom's capital that first day.

As he looked, his eyes fell upon the daughter of the village baker.

She was neither plain nor pretty, but next to her, the whole world faded to nothing. In the flutter of three beats of his heart, the King, who had withstood the battlefields and brutalities of war, was conquered.

So he met his red-blooded queen.

Such discoveries of true love occurred across the land, in every kingdom. Unwittingly, a bridge of harmony and peace was built between the two worlds. True love conquered the draw of wild magic. Human hearts ceased their greed. It cemented each kingdom's place in the treaty because two rulers, united in love, longed for nothing more than to spend the rest of their days content in one another's company.

But the day came when the Faerie King Stephan and his queen gave birth to a son. His tiny, mortal body, an unnatural vessel for the power of the fae, sang out with wild magic as strongly as if he had stolen it from his faerie cousins. The King and the Queen watched in horror as he grew, biding their time, knowing that they would one day have to make that terrible decision to end their child's life for the sake of the world.

The child grew to be a young man, and though the wild magic still surrounded him with intoxicating glamour, his parents could not bring themselves to kill him, for his heart was kind and his intentions pure.

On the eve of his sixteenth birthday, the King and Queen held a ball for their son. Standing on the dance floor, a young woman curtsied before the Prince. The stories said that time stood still as the two gazed upon one another and that the heavens smiled as their lips touched. The power of true love's first kiss transformed the wild magic in the Prince's veins to the ordered elemental magic of the purest of fae. The treaty's requirement for a blue-blooded faerie upon the throne was fulfilled, and the Prince ruled with wisdom and grace till the end of his days.

But over the years, heirs began to marry for strategic might and not love. The blue blood thinned to red as the memory of the treaty faded into legend. The fae were seen once more as mere animals with powers that should be owned and controlled. The day came when six of the Kingdoms united to claim that which they thought could be taken.

Driven back, mankind was reminded by the faerie that all legends were based in truth.

From this second terrible battle came the first Woodcutter, whose memory was as old as the trees. The borders were redrawn so that the Twelve Kingdoms intersected in the Woodcutter's Wood. The Woodcutter was to be an ambassador between the mortal and immortal worlds. He pledged to remember the treaty, pledged to remind the Twelve Kingdoms of their obligations. He was to be a protector that ensured never more than half the Kingdoms thirsted for power, for if that balance ever tipped and seven Kingdoms turned to the dark hunger, there was nothing he, nor any Woodcutter, could do to stave off the massacre.

In the Vanishing House, the Woodcutter had counted six Princes. Six Princes of six Kingdoms. There had been so much dust, more than anything that would come freely given. The blood of the Gentleman had run blue, but with enough magic, any human could turn for a while.

A cold chill crept up the Woodcutter's back as Snow White's words came back to him about the pixies being harvested in a moving castle.

Pixies touching the ground...

There are things human ears should never have to hear.

There was an urgency to his footfalls as he continued on his way.

CHAPTER 22

A slender lad, all elbows and knees, sat on a stump by the road. His blue doublet was worn and faded. His short, curly mop of hair was hidden beneath a floppy hat. His face was swollen and red as he hastily wiped the tears from his cheeks, pretending that he belonged all alone in the middle of the Wood.

The Woodcutter stopped before the boy. The lad seemed the rough and tumble sort, just on the edge of adulthood when immortality seemed certain and the whole world was at his feet.

The Woodcutter asked, "Why do you cry, boy?"

The boy's voice had not quite kept pace with the rest of his body, and he replied in a voice just a few notes too high, "I'm lost."

He spoke with a thick peasant's accent, but his face was too youthful for the life a peasant would have led. In fact, his face was too interesting for any pure-blooded human.

"Where did you come from?" asked the Woodcutter, his senses prickling.

"I don't know," said the boy. "I was in one place, and now I'm here."

The Woodcutter took off his pack and rubbed his sore shoulders. "My back is not as it once was. You seem young and strong. If you carry my pack, you may travel with me."

The boy wiped his nose warily but did not move toward the Woodcutter.

The Woodcutter had been cautious and had obeyed the faerie rules of allowing true blue bloods to find their way. He had obeyed the rules, and the child dressed in a red cape was dead. He would not be haunted by another corpse. He looked up at the darkening sky. "There are things that walk in the night that you should not face alone."

The boy's face drained of color. A stick fell noisily from a nearby tree and the boy spun as if a ghost were at his back. The Woodcutter shook his head at the tree and the tree shifted apologetically for the dramatics. The Woodcutter held out his pack and the boy grudgingly took it, falling in step behind the Woodcutter as they continued deeper into the Wood.

The wind tasted of rain.

The Woodcutter raised his nose to the air and inhaled the scent of the trees as they opened themselves for a cool evening drink.

The forest in this part of the Wood was different than elsewhere. Moss and ferns grew abundantly. The pulp of the trees was rust colored, and the trees grew so tall they almost disappeared in the clouds.

The wind scolded him like a wizened mother, pushing at the Woodcutter's back and telling him that he should find shelter.

The Woodcutter's eyes fell upon a hollow in one of the trees. Struck by lightning, the inside had burned away but had left the exterior intact and alive. There was just enough room for two.

The Woodcutter crawled in and the boy followed just as the first drops began to fall.

The Woodcutter took out a blanket his wife had rolled into his pack and handed it to the boy. Then he tucked up the collar of his coat and settled in for the night.

The boy just sniffled.

CHAPTER 23

The Woodcutter was awake in an instant.

The rain had stopped.

The boy was fast asleep, his head tilted back at an awkward angle.

But something was wrong.

The Woodcutter could feel it in his bones, even before the trees began to whisper, *Quiet...quiet...*

He crawled to the entrance and tried to see out into the night.

He could hear the snuffling grunts of an animal, a large creature tracking something through the brush.

The Woodcutter looked at the boy sleeping behind him. He placed his hand upon his final Ax. He waited as the footsteps grew closer.

A creature of silver stepped into the clearing. His ears were pricked, and his mastiff-like snout tasted the air. He muscles rippled like mercury. Walking on four legs, his shoulders stood as tall as a man's chest. A halo of blue radiated from him. His eyes were mirrors, lacking pupils, and shone gray in the night.

Odin's rogue hellhound.

The Beast.

The Woodcutter felt the boy behind him wake with a start.

He reached back and grabbed the boy's ankle, hoping he would understand to stay silent.

The hellhound's head jerked in their direction. The Beast lowered his nose to the ground and began creeping their way.

The Woodcutter placed his hands upon the opening of the tree and closed his eyes. He whispered a wish to the tree, and the spell took hold.

The Beast leapt, attracted by the movement, but when he reached the base of the redwood, all he found was wood and bark.

The Woodcutter still stood at the opening, mere inches from the Beast, but the spell had created a mirage that the hollow tree was solid. The spells he used were elemental, not the wild magic of the dark knives or unclaimed hearts that seemed to call the Beast.

The Beast snuffed and dug at the tree, but the spell did not give up its secret. The Beast let out a sneeze before padding away. As the last of the hellhound's blue aura disappeared deep into the Wood, the Woodcutter relaxed.

"What was that?" the boy asked.

"A hellhound," said the Woodcutter.

The boy shifted uncomfortably. "Can you kill it?"

"I shall try sometime when I am by myself." The Woodcutter looked back at the boy. "I would hate to leave you alone with it."

The Woodcutter released the spell and settled back against the inside of the tree. "Now, can you tell me why this beast has picked you as his prey?"

The boy seemed to size up the Woodcutter, as if weighing his character. "My name is Rapunzel."

He took off his hat, and the Woodcutter saw it was a she, not a he, who sat beside him. She ran her fingers through her short, curly hair and then held out her hand.

Rapunzel.

A sense filled the Woodcutter's being, a sense that there was something terribly wrong as he stared at her closely shorn hair.

He took her hand delicately in his rough and calloused own. "Woodcutter," he replied.

They stood for a moment more.

"Perhaps now you remember how you came to the crossroads?" he suggested.

"There is a witch…" Rapunzel stopped and then began again. "My parents weren't supposed to have a baby, but my father stole some watercress from a witch's garden. The witch said she would take me as payment for the greens." She looked at the Woodcutter proudly. "We've been gypsies since before the day I was born. I look like a boy to fool the witch."

"Where are your parents now?"

"I don't know." She shrugged as she scratched her leg, but a small tremor in her voice gave away her worry. "I went to bed the night before last and woke at the crossroads where you found me."

The girl with glass slippers…

The princes in the Vanishing House…

Rapunzel shivered, but not from the chill in the air. "Why was he tracking me?"

Even in the darkness of the tree, she seemed to shine.

"Because you are special, young one."

Rapunzel laughed. "You're mistaken."

But he was not. There had been something unusual about the watercress her mother had eaten while pregnant with this child, he was sure of it.

"Have you ever nicked your finger?" asked the Woodcutter.

"Sure," she replied.

"What color was your blood?"

"Blue. Like everybody's."

"Not like everybody's."

Rapunzel pointed at the veins in her arm. "Everyone has blue."

The Woodcutter shook his head. "That is not how these things work."

"You're saying my blood is a strange color and so that creature wants to eat me?"

The Woodcutter wanted to deny it, but he could not.

So he said nothing.

She became quiet. "You're serious." She stood, their hideaway in the tree suddenly becoming too small. "So what do we do? Run for eternity?"

"We could," said the Woodcutter.

"I just want to go home."

"You would not be safe. You were brought to the Wood once. Whoever brought you here would most likely bring you once again."

"I was brought to the Wood to be food for some hellhound." She swayed and gripped her sides with her arms as she became desperate. "You have to help me. You have to find a way to keep me safe."

Son...

His father's voice...

It seemed like only yesterday they had stood in the Wood together.

Son...

He pushed it back.

Son, there will be a day that you will need refuge...

He pushed away the memory of what happened next.

"There is a tower..." the Woodcutter said.

She looked at him incredulously. "A tower?"

"You will be safe until I find the Crone."

"The Crone?"

"I have been told she knows how to defeat a hellhound."

"You would leave me alone while you wander off to seek out some crone?" Rapunzel's voice hit a strained pitch.

The Woodcutter calmly said, "Or we could walk for eternity and hope we never cross paths with the Beast."

Rapunzel's mouth opened. And then closed again.

The Woodcutter looked toward where the Beast last walked. "We would best put some distance between us and this place."

The Woodcutter crawled out of the tree and patted the rough bark. "Thank you, my friend. Know that my ax has never been tainted by unwilling sap and so it shall always be."

The leaves of the hollow tree seemed to rustle, warily, but in understanding.

The Woodcutter held out his hand to Rapunzel and helped her to her feet.

They walked in the opposite direction of the Beast for the rest of the night, until the sky slowly faded from deep blue to light pink.

As the sun kissed the morning, they reached the clearing. The tower had no windows or doors, only a single balcony forty feet above the ground.

Rapunzel held out her hand to the Woodcutter. "Promise to come back for me?"

The Woodcutter took her tiny fingers in his palm. "I promise."

He turned toward the trees, toward their long strips of bark, knowing he must ask them for a sacrifice to create a rope to climb to the top of the tower.

But before the wish could escape his lips, Rapunzel was already several feet off the ground, scaling the sheer sides of the building.

"Do not injure yourself!" he cried out in alarm.

She looked over her shoulder and smiled. "I have always been good at climbing."

He watched as those tiny fingers found holds in the wall of the tower, as her feet found an impossible ledge, as she climbed higher and higher. She finally pulled herself over the balcony into the only window.

He stood below, wondering if he had done right to bring her, to leave her in the tower by herself, but the glowing form of the hellhound crept into the back of his mind, the hellhound who had killed so many already.

Suddenly the Woodcutter heard the sound of scuffling and heard Rapunzel's terrified cry.

"Rapunzel!" he shouted as he looked for those holds that would carry him up the sheer blocks.

"Rapunzel!" he cried as the scuffling abruptly stopped.

Silence.

Silence.

His heart seemed to stop beating in that silence of a thousand years.

"It's all right!" she called down. "There is someone else here."

His heart was in his throat. "Who?"

Her voice softened.

And a warm buzz ran its way through the Woodcutter's veins.

"A man."

A man.

She and the man appeared on the balcony, their gaze oddly intent.

Wild magic finding its path.

Wild magic finding its home.

"I am Prince Martin," the tawny-headed man called down. A ladder was thrown over the balcony and the two descended.

CHAPTER 24

Frog songs filled the night and a crackling fire warmed their camp. The three had finished dinner and the conversation had slowed to silence. Rapunzel stepped out of the light and Prince Martin excused himself.

The Woodcutter watched the flames as they licked and popped in the air.

He lit his pipe.

You shall have your princes, but not here. Go find them, dog.

The words of the strange Gentleman echoed in his memory.

Go find them.

The Woodcutter tried not to listen to the breathy feminine giggles coming from the forest and the lower rumbling response.

Go find them.

Prince Martin, heir to the Eighth Kingdom, said he had gone on an overnight hunting trip. He said he went to sleep with his party, but woke in the tower. He had no memory of the Vanishing House, but the Woodcutter remembered Prince Martin's face. He had carried a tray of silver dust boxes.

The Woodcutter gazed at the rings of smoke from his pipe.

Powerful magic. Princes. Princesses. Hellhounds...

A clap of thunder interrupted the Woodcutter's thoughts as lightning lit up the sky.

The cry of the hellhound rang out into the night.

He jumped from his seat, Ax in hand.

Prince Martin and Rapunzel ran back. Prince Martin's sword was drawn and Rapunzel clung to his side.

The Woodcutter smiled and lowered his weapon.

Of course.

"You kissed her," the Woodcutter said.

The bright flush to Rapunzel's cheeks told him the answer.

Prince Martin looked at him threateningly. "And what if I did?"

The Woodcutter laughed a powerful laugh that calmed the wind, a laugh that seemed to part the phantom clouds until the moon shone bright once more, a laugh that seemed to set everything right.

"True love's first kiss."

The young couple looked at one another.

Yes, true love's first kiss.

"The spell has been broken," said the Woodcutter. He sheathed the Platinum Ax. "The hellhound that stalked you will have lost your scent, for you are no longer that which you were and will forever be more than you ever thought possible.

"In losing yourself to one another, you have won. The blood of the fae within your veins has been tamed and you have fulfilled your role in the treaty—for you have chosen to love.

"The Wood shall now grant you safe passage to your home. Whatever danger you were once in has now passed. Tomorrow, Prince Martin, no matter what direction you travel, you shall arrive in your kingdom by sundown. There you shall wed your Rapunzel, and together you shall live happily ever after."

The couple smiled curiously at one another.

The Woodcutter rose to retire for the night and leave the young couple to discovery. He knew they no longer needed him, for wild magic does not meddle with the hearts of those who have tamed it with love true.

For true love conquers all.

CHAPTER 25

He left them in the morning, parting with them at a crossroads. A dappled gray horse stood as if waiting—which he was.

Prince Martin slid his hand along the horse's neck. "Why, it's Pacer! I haven't seen him since the hunting trip…" His voice trailed off and he looked at the Woodcutter worriedly.

"Your horse has been kept well by the Wood and is free of all enchantments. Give him his head and ride steadily on. You shall be home before nightfall," said the Woodcutter.

He was almost telling the truth.

As Prince Martin helped Rapunzel mount, the horse looked back at the Woodcutter.

And winked.

The Woodcutter hid his smile in his beard.

An animal does not spend so many days eating the foods of the fae without some effect.

"We thank you, Woodcutter, for your kindness," Prince Martin began.

"We shall never forget…" Rapunzel continued.

The Woodcutter was about to wave them away…

But the trees began to whisper, began to whisper to him of a duty...

He closed his eyes. He opened his ears. He allowed his mouth to be the mouth of the Wood.

"Repay the kindness you have received by allowing your kingdom to be a friend to these Woods. Harm not the trees or the animals. Harm not the fae. And you shall travel its paths with no fear," said the words that came out.

Prince Martin declared, "So shall it be done by ourselves and our descendants. You shall always be welcomed and heralded as a friend whenever you visit the Eighth Kingdom."

The Woodcutter opened his eyes, and the trees murmured their thanks.

"Travel well, my friends," said the Woodcutter.

He watched them as they rode out of sight.

CHAPTER 26

The water was cold and deep.

It had started off at his ankles, but soon was to his thighs and then his waist and then deeper.

The roots of the mangroves were giant fingers soaking in a bowl of pale-brown water. The thick fog of the flooded forest masked his view. A bird cried overhead.

He pushed aside a stick as it floated toward him. His foot slipped upon a rock and the water rose to his neck. His arms held his pack tightly upon his head as he looked up at the soft, twinkling lights radiating from the tops of the trees.

Faerie light.

Pixies congregated freely in this deep, hidden corner of the Wood. Their gentle pinpricks would dart together and then dart off again to another tree. Their musical speech floated down like tiny bells. Tiny bells that seemed to laugh...

The tiny foot hitting the earth...

His mind revolted and pushed the memory away.

"Woodcutter..."

The voice shot from tree to tree, echoing high in the branches.

"Woodcutter…"

He hated traveling at dusk, when the ordered magic of the day made way for the wild magic of night. His hand secretly gripped the handle of the Platinum Ax.

"Woodcutter…" came the voice again.

"Who calls my name?" he asked.

The tinkling of female laughter shook the leaves of the trees.

"Who?" he called.

The whole forest shook as the laughter seemed to gather in the arms of a giant mangrove tree before him. The sound wrapped from the base and climbed up the trunk, and as it touched the highest bough, a mighty cracking sound cut across the forest. Like a sleepy kitten uncurling in a sunbeam, the tree opened, revealing a radiant woman of glowing pink, ungarbed, but not indecent. The dryad was art and life. Her voice was deep and earthy as she reached an impossibly slender hand to him.

"Woodcutter, hast thou ever spilt the sap of an unwilling tree?" she asked.

The water flowing about him became warm and still. A sense of peace and contentment washed over the Woodcutter as he gazed upon her face.

The Woodcutter bowed his head.

"Never, Mother Dryad," he said. "My ax remains virgin and true."

She smiled quietly. "Word of thy deeds has reached our ears."

The trunks of ten…twenty…thirty…mangroves opened, revealing their hidden, glowing mistresses.

The Mother Dryad motioned to her sisters. "We have heard of thy quest to find the Crone and will grant thee safe passage through our grove."

"Sister," whispered one of the creatures, "the pixies."

The trees' branches shook anxiously.

"The pixies…" they whispered urgently.

The Woodcutter offered, "Mother Dryad, I have heard of terrible deeds, of pixies touching the earth."

The trees shook in horror, and the lights of the dryads dimmed sadly.

"They came to our grove," said a green dryad as she pointed to the top of her tree. The top still sparkled, but not as brightly as the tree beside her.

"They came and...kidnapped..."

"They spilled innocent sap..."

"Stole the fae..."

The pink Mother Dryad held up a hand to silence them as the dryads spoke at once, but they would not be stilled and continued.

"We grow here, sisters of the Mother Dryad, and we may not leave. But our daughter pixies..."

"Robbed of their magic..."

"Touching the earth..."

The Mother Dryad's face was haunted in pain as her sisters' voices rose. Her eyes locked upon the Woodcutter. "Each atrocity reverberates to our very roots."

"The stolen magic steals from us our strength..."

"Help us!"

"We cannot leave our trees..."

"But you can..."

The feminine voices climbed, pleading in chorus, "We shall aid your journey to the Crone if you will save our daughters."

The Woodcutter held up his hand and the trees fell silent.

"I am your servant," he said.

The Mother Dryad smiled hopefully as a single tear drifted down her pink cheek. She clasped her hands together and caught the tear as it fell. When she opened her hands, three round seeds glowed in her palm.

She tossed them gently to the Woodcutter, and they arced through the air, a trail of gold following them in the dark.

He caught them in his mighty fist.

"Thou shalt know what to do with them," said the Mother Dryad.

You shall know, the trees spoke.

The Mother Dryad swept her hand before her, and a branch from her tree dipped into the water.

The Woodcutter felt the wood against his back and felt himself lifted from the flood.

"We grant thee safe passage," said the Mother Dryad.

Another bough came forward, cradling him as the trees transferred his body from one to the next.

"Remember your promise."

The trunks began closing behind him. The eyes of the pink dryad never left his face until the final moment of the bark's embrace.

Swiftly the trees moved him through the swamp, high above the chill of the water.

A small light darted curiously to his face. The newborn pixie was the size of his thumb and as round as a baby chick. Its large black eyes studied the Woodcutter before laughing and darting away.

The pixie's laugh tickled its way down the Woodcutter's body, warming and wiggling as it went. It sloughed away all sorrow. It carried away all worry. The Woodcutter's mouth spread into a wide grin, and he leaned his head back, laughing deep from his belly.

The lights in the trees glittered back in response, the tinkling sound of the fae filling the night.

The Woodcutter passed by another treetop. Tucked within the knots and indentations of the wood was a pixie nursery. Curled in blankets of leaves, snuggled into the gentle support of the wood like pussy willows, the pixies blossomed and grew. As the Woodcutter laughed, the baby pixies' eyes opened and they were awake like Christmas morning.

They rose from their beds and brushed up against the Wood-cutter, touching his hair and wondering at his buttons, even as the trees tried to shoo them back to bed.

And then he passed a tree of bleached-white wood, and all the pixies withdrew. A forgotten moth drifted through the empty branches. The nursery had been robbed, and the tree's dryad was dead. The silence and emptiness of that tree burned itself into his mind.

He would not forget his promise to the trees.

He traveled for hours, finally falling asleep in the gentle movement, like a child cradled in a parent's arms.

He woke as his feet touched the marshy ground at the edge of the Wood.

The sun was rising.

CHAPTER 27

The morning haze did not burn off in the midday sun.

The trees had become sparse, and his skin crawled.

He did not like the world without the dappled shadows from the sun filtering through the leaves. He did not like the size of the sky.

Bogs lay to the right and to the left. The dirt trails of the forest had been replaced by a wooden road, the logs laid upon the soggy peat.

His shoulders ached, and he longed for his wife's fingers to work out the knots.

He shifted his pack.

Too long, his feet seemed to patter. *Too long*, he had been away. *Too long.*

The faint clank of a cowbell was the first warning that he was not alone.

A man's voice pointlessly instructed, "Gitup," to the sound of wheels and hooves.

The Peddler's wagon emerged from the mist, red and blue, hitched to a single ox. The Peddler pulled back on the reins and pressed the brake down with his foot.

He and the Woodcutter regarded one another.

A heron cried.

"Well, there, sir. I didn't seem to think I'd find a fellow out these parts." The Peddler smiled as he pushed back his hat. "You wouldn't be in the market for a…"

The Peddler looked at the Woodcutter, trying to size him up.

"I suppose I might have some items that might interest you. Why don't you stop a spell with me? I'll brew some coffee and we can talk some business."

The Woodcutter said nothing.

The Peddler shifted uncomfortably in the silence. "Of course, if you prefer something stronger, well, I might be able to find something to suit your taste. Nothing like a little dust to relax a fellow."

The Woodcutter held up his hand. "No dust. Plain coffee would be fine."

The Peddler slapped his thigh. "There we go. Thought the cat got your tongue, there."

He turned around and ducked his head into a small doorway in the cart. He pulled out a large coffee mill and gave the Woodcutter a wink.

As he turned the handle, instead of coffee grounds, a fire fell from the mill. Then a grill. Then a steaming coffeepot and two full cups, two armchairs and a table.

Then the Peddler stopped grinding.

"That should do it," he said.

The Peddler hopped off the cart and walked over to the coffee. He picked up one of the cups and handed it to the Woodcutter. "Dust free, just as promised."

The Woodcutter took the coffee cup and smelled it cautiously before raising it to his lips.

The Peddler laid his finger on the side of his nose. "You have no idea how glad I am, too. Far too many people looking for dust, if you ask me."

He sat in the armchair. "Come, rest your feet. I promise you there is no place to sit for the next fifty miles."

The Woodcutter accepted his invitation.

"So, do you have a name there, sir?"

"I am called Woodcutter."

The Peddler blew the steam from the coffee and took a tentative sip. He smacked his lips in appreciation. "Fair enough. So, what brings you out these parts?"

"I am looking for the Crone."

"Never heard of her. Where's she live?"

"I am not sure."

The Peddler laughed. "Well, that does make things a bit more difficult. How are the roads ahead?"

The Woodcutter looked back where he had come from. "You would do best not to enter the Wood. Strange things are afoot."

The Peddler's eyes were at once sharp. "There are strange things all over."

"Not like this."

The Peddler leapt to his feet, his eyes upon the Woodcutter's Ax. "While you finish your drink, perhaps I can interest you in some wares for your coming journey."

He went to the back of the wagon and pulled out a beautiful ax that glistened in the gray light. Its handle was stout and curved for the perfect grip.

"With a name like Woodcutter, you perhaps might be in the market for this beauty."

As the Peddler brought the ax closer, the Woodcutter winced.

He could hear its cries, the cry of the innocent wood whose sap had been unwillingly spilled.

A thousand voices screamed.

"I have no use for such a thing," said the Woodcutter.

The Peddler stopped shrewdly. "But such a fine ax…Why, a gentleman like yourself sure could use a backup instrument for your trade."

The Woodcutter swallowed down the bile rising in his throat. "Put it away, Peddler. Otherwise our time together is done."

The Peddler tucked the ax back into his cart. "I thought so."

He returned to the Woodcutter, holding a small object wrapped in a handkerchief. "I believe this is for you."

The Peddler pulled back the corner of the cloth. Gasping in his palm was a small pixie whose eyes opened and shut, unable to focus.

The Woodcutter's hand was immediately upon his Ax.

The Peddler did not notice. His eyes were trained upon the tiny creature. "I scooped it up as it fell from the air. It was so close to touching the ground."

He looked at the Woodcutter. Shadows played upon his face. He was a man haunted, a man who knew what it meant when a pixie touched the earth.

He gently transferred the bundle into the Woodcutter's hands. "You winced at that ax...I figure maybe, so close to the trees, some of those stories my mother once told me might be true. Figure maybe you might know someone who could help."

The pixie smiled at the Woodcutter, feeble and weak.

And the Woodcutter knew. He knew that the pixie would not last the journey to the Wood, would not last long enough to reach a tree whose heart was pure enough to heal the life force that had been drained.

He reached down and willingly nicked his thumb upon his father's ax.

But instead of blood, something else flowed.

Clear.

Sticky.

He held his finger, gashed willingly to allow the sap to flow to the mouth of the fae.

The pixie drank hungrily.

And then fell asleep.

The Peddler stepped back, all cunningness gone. Only fear remained as he said, "I have met many strange men upon my journey…"

The Woodcutter looked at him. "And so you have today."

"What make of man are you?"

The Woodcutter knew he could not deny the clear blood that seeped from the wound. He looked down at the small sprite that had forced him to reveal his true face. "I am one with the trees, a cutting of my father, and of his father, and of his father before him. I was born of the earth and not the womb."

The Peddler whistled low and with wonder. "A walking, talking wood cutting. Well, I thought I had seen everything."

The Woodcutter looked at him seriously. "Do not venture into the Wood, my friend. The danger is great."

The Peddler took out the coffee grinder once more and began turning the crank in reverse. The objects flew through the air and disappeared back into the grinder's mouth.

"I'll take your word for it."

The Woodcutter felt something in his pocket grow heavy. "I must give you payment for this little one."

He pulled out the three seeds and poured them into the Peddler's palm.

"Now what am I going to do with three seeds?"

"They are magic," said the Woodcutter.

The Peddler turned them over in his hand. "Seeds, you say? They look a bit like beans. Maybe I'll get someone to trade me a cow for them or something."

He laughed hard at his joke.

"Well, hardly seems fair, trading one injured pixie for three magic…beans. Seems I'm still in your debt." He put his finger to his nose. "One pixie for one bean. How about I pass you some information for that second bean?"

The Woodcutter nodded.

The Peddler pointed down the wooden road. "You'll come to an intersection ahead. Make sure to take the left-hand fork or go straight ahead. There's an odd house to the right, an odd house with an odder group of people. I went in thinking the kitchen staff might be interested in something I had to sell, but instead I found this little one, practically drained. Keep to your left or straight ahead. You don't need to be venturing to your right. Beyond that house is a village and a sorry kingdom that has been nothing since the Princess disappeared."

The Woodcutter looked at him sharply. "Disappeared?"

"Disappeared. She was a sad little thing. Hadn't smiled in years. The King said anyone that could make her smile, why, he could marry her, sure thing. But one day she went to bed, and the next day she was gone. The King and Queen went mad. Threw themselves from a cliff. Can't say I blame them, but the town's in a mess as they try to find an heir from all the people walking around with only red blood."

The Woodcutter felt the pixie stir.

The Peddler wiped his face with a red handkerchief. "Meanwhile, some boy came through carrying a golden goose, and everyone who tries to touch the boy gets stuck. Don't know if they ever found a way out."

The Peddler rolled the seeds in his palm. "Well, seems that I still owe you one more thing to pay off the balance for…these."

He went to his wagon and closed his eyes. He took a giant breath and allowed his hands to rest upon an object.

"I suppose this is for you," he said. It was a medium-sized package. "I guess you shouldn't open it until you're supposed to."

The Woodcutter nodded and placed it inside his pack.

The Peddler climbed up into the seat of his cart. "Travel well, Woodcutter."

"Travel well, Peddler."

"Well traded, my friend! Well traded!" he cried as his cart and the cowbell disappeared into the mist.

CHAPTER 28

The Woodcutter went straight at the crossroads. The chosen path left the Twelve Kingdoms, but provided a shortcut to the far side of the Wood. He felt the Kingdom end and the duchy begin the moment he stepped foot across the border. The colors were duller and the shadows were without mystery. It was a land without magic.

It was the Land of the Pure Ordinary.

The lowlands were no place for wheat fields and corn. The saturated peat rotted the roots of any plant besides the tall grasses and rice paddies. The natural iron that filled the bogs repelled any magic that tried to take hold.

Which is why he was startled when he first saw the butterfly.

Its wings were beating slowly in the mud. It was made of gold and encrusted with jewels. The Woodcutter bent down and lifted it from the mire, brushing off the filth as best he could. The butterfly rested for a moment and then took off, limping through the air toward the Wood.

The Woodcutter wiped his hands upon his trousers and watched it as it flew away.

The bejeweled butterfly was far from its home. It was far from the boundary of the Twelve Kingdoms and deep in the Land of the Ordinary for a butterfly.

It was not unheard of, but odd.

The Woodcutter turned back to the road, although the hollow wind made him uncomfortable and he did not like to be without the counsel of the trees.

Hours later, he saw before him a low-rising hill, which seated a stone city where the Duke of Plainness made his home.

The Woodcutter walked through the gates to look for a place to spend the night.

The city was bustling. A full cart of hay rumbled down the narrow street, making its way to market. The Woodcutter fell in behind, allowing the ox to part the crowds and lead him to the center of the city. As the buildings opened up to the central square, the Woodcutter stepped aside to view the area.

He stopped.

Every booth was filled with spinning wheels and hay. Every merchant had pushed aside his regular wares to make room.

The Woodcutter walked between the towers of spindles as people eagerly toted away the machines. He walked past a doctor hawking, "An elixir! An elixir to mend your twisted bones!" and past large bales people used to fill their carts.

He would have expected such behavior in the Twelve Kingdoms, but not in the other world, not in the Land of the Ordinary.

A water fountain was surrounded by a group of young ladies who gaped at something in the water and giggled.

The Woodcutter gently pushed his way to the front.

At the edge of the fountain sat a large frog.

The frog regarded the Woodcutter, and the Woodcutter regarded the frog.

And then the frog croaked, "Give me a kiss and I will turn into a prince."

But the Woodcutter would not be fooled.

A girl with a straw-colored plait that hung down her back looked at the Woodcutter. "He says that, but no matter how many times I kiss him, he stays a frog."

The frog gave the Woodcutter a wink.

The Woodcutter said to the girls as he turned to walk away, "The frog lies."

The Woodcutter made his way directly toward the nearest village pub. There was at least one place in every town where information flowed freely, and in the Duchy of Plainness, it came beneath a wooden sign bearing a red fox.

The villagers were speaking loudly as he entered. One angrily spat, "Do you believe such madness?"

The Woodcutter walked past and settled himself at a table nearby.

A tavern keeper in a dirty gray smock came over and placed a meal and a drink before the Woodcutter. The Woodcutter placed two wooden coins upon the table. The tavern keeper eyed them warily but deposited them in a purse around his waist. As he moved to leave, the Woodcutter caught his sleeve. The tavern keeper glared at the Woodcutter but did not walk away.

"I am a stranger to this land," the Woodcutter said. "And I have seen some strange things today. Tell me, what causes the people here to buy spinning wheels and bales of hay?"

The tavern keeper remained silent.

The Woodcutter placed another coin upon the table.

The man scooped it up and then said, "Seems the Duke has gone mad. Swears he met a girl who could spin straw into gold. She ran off, and now he says she's been disguised by evil forces and he'll marry whatever girl can spin gold out of a wheel. He's calling them in by the dozens each day, just sitting them in front of him and asking them to spin. A whole lot of nonsense, if you ask me."

The Woodcutter looked at him sharply. "I did not think such things happened around these parts."

The tavern keeper grumbled angrily, "'Twas a strange winter. We had snow, but the snow was warm. Odd things started happening, and just when the strangeness started to fade away, the snow would come back and the whole nonsense returned."

"I spoke with a frog in the town fountain..."

The tavern keeper pointed at the Woodcutter. "This is what I'm talking about. Frogs that talk and mice that sing. If I wanted magic, I'd've stayed in that infernal Kingdom. But a body wants some peace and quiet and finally finds a place without that fae racket and what happens? Talking frogs."

The tavern keeper leaned his face in close to the Woodcutter's. His breath reeked of stale beer. "If you ask me, it reminds me of when those pixies used to go running through the towns on Midsummer's Eve. Everything is set to wrong here. Everything."

The pixie in the Woodcutter's coat pocket shuddered.

The tavern keeper took an empty plate from a side table. "But I say it's shameful, those faerie folk coming over here and bothering us when we want nothing to do with their kind. You'd think they were trying to turn us on to magic. But the iron in our soul shall keep us safe from them. You mark my word. Their magic doesn't belong here, and we shall not be made their slaves."

The Woodcutter had lost his appetite. He pushed away the plate and stood. "Thank you for the information." He threw the tavern keeper another coin. "I hope your days are magic-free."

The tavern keeper grunted at him and stalked back into the kitchen.

The Woodcutter entered the inn and was greeted by a slender woman with hair streaked with iron gray. He followed her into the great room and noticed a young girl playing with some bits of straw by the hearth. Her neck held her head at an odd angle, and her legs twisted into clawed feet. Her red hair was the color of the flames.

"Poor duck," her mother clucked as she saw the Woodcutter look at the child. "Pines away for the Duke. I keep telling her all she has to do is learn how to spin the straw into gold and he'll see she is a beautiful princess, but she won't listen to her mother. They never do."

The woman continued on to the stairway.

The girl looked at the Woodcutter, and the power of her gaze made him step back.

There was something too interesting about her face.

The pixie stirred as the blue blood of the girl called out. The fae always recognize a familiar.

But there was something horribly twisted about this glamour.

The girl turned back to the fire, and the Woodcutter realized he had been holding his breath.

A blue blood in the inn. The glamour was not upon her mother, and the Woodcutter wondered how it came to be.

CHAPTER 29

The Woodcutter opened his eyes and stared at the thatched ceiling above him. He rolled to his side. The pixie lay fast asleep upon a roughly hewn table by his bed. Its breathing was still shallow. It needed to get to the Wood.

The Woodcutter yearned to leave at once for the safety and comfort of his trees.

He sat up upon the edge of the mattress, his joints cracking and popping. He was exhausted despite the full night's rest. His fingers found their way to his beard, stroking his whiskers absentmindedly. He lifted the flap from his pack and pulled out his pipe.

The border between the worlds of magic and ordinary was marked where the magic ended. By default, if the magic continued, the land became the jurisdiction of the fae.

There were too many strange things going on in the duchy. The magic was not natural. He could feel it. He knew that the iron in the land would eventually chase the magic away, but until then, it fell upon the duties of the position of Woodcutter to inform the Duke of the treaty. The Duke needed to know what was going on.

The Woodcutter tapped out his pipe resolutely and gently tucked the pixie into his vest, whispering a quiet promise that they would return to the old growth soon.

The room was full of people waiting for an audience with the Duke. The hall dripped with coats of arms and formal tapestries. Each person carried a spinning wheel and sat with a daughter of eligible age.

The Woodcutter settled himself beneath a tall window and leaned against the stone frame.

Outside, the sky was covered in a sheet of clouds, casting the world in tones of gray.

Two large wooden doors swung open and a blustering man shouted as he and his daughter were forcibly pushed out. "She could spin gold at home! Give her a chance! She was only frightened!"

The doors closed behind them with a boom.

The man hurled the spinning wheel he carried against the wall, dashing it to pieces. He grabbed his daughter violently by the arm. "Well, there you have it. You had your chance. Now you'll be nothing but a goose girl till the end of your days."

The girl wept as her father dragged her out of the room.

A bony advisor dressed in green velvet came out of double doors carrying a long scroll in one hand and a plume darkened by ink in the other. His fringe of white hair stood up wildly. He did not look up as he read the next name from the list. "Maid Adamson and escort."

A plump, freckled girl and her mother picked up their drop spindle and followed the advisor into the audience chamber.

They emerged shortly. The mother stroked her daughter's shoulders. "Even if you could spin straw into gold, we wouldn't waste such a gift on a mere duke. Why, we would have sent you to the King…"

Her voice trailed off as they walked away.

The Woodcutter watched as girl after girl stepped hopefully into the room, and each stepped out moments later, defeated.

Finally the Woodcutter was the only one left.

The advisor stepped out, nose still in the scroll. "All eligible maidens..." He looked up and saw that only the Woodcutter remained.

"Oh," said the advisor. He looked at his scroll. "I am afraid you are not on my list."

The Woodcutter stood. "I believe I can be of assistance to the Duke."

The advisor stuttered, "Well...You are not on the list...But you say you are able to help. Oh my. Oh my, my, my. This is out of order, but perhaps..." He looked at the Woodcutter, trying to size up his character. "My, my, my. I suppose we should see."

He beckoned to the Woodcutter to follow.

A very sad man sat at an ornate desk in the center of the room. The Duke's black curls only emphasized the dark circles under his bloodshot eyes. The Duke looked up at the Woodcutter in confusion.

The advisor explained, "This man says that he can help locate the woman. I thought that, perhaps, since all of the girls have left for the day, perhaps it would be best if you granted him an audience..."

The Duke nodded and waved away the advisor, who backed submissively out of the room.

The Woodcutter could feel the longing in the air, could smell the wildness that came when two souls meant for one another were parted.

He knew it was true love.

"I shall help you," stated the Woodcutter.

"And what can you do to help me?" asked the Duke, discouragement coloring his voice.

"You would be surprised," said the Woodcutter. He stepped closer to the table. "Tell me about your love and I shall help you find her."

The Duke stood wearily. "Such promises... I am so tired of promises..." He spread his hands toward the Woodcutter and said, "Her name is Maid Maleen. She was from the Twelve Kingdoms, which I know was wrong, but when I first saw her in the village square, I knew she was my true love."

The Woodcutter asked, "But what of her disappearance?"

The Duke heaved a sigh as if his heart had been cleft in twain. "Her father, thinking I would not marry someone below my rank, swore to my advisor that she could spin gold out of straw."

The Duke began pacing, his words coming faster. "My advisor, unbeknownst to me, shut her in a prison cell with a bale of straw and a spinning wheel. I do not know what he said to her, but come the morning, that bale had been replaced by gold coins. So my advisor kept her there another night. The next morning, the room was once more filled with golden coins. But when he tried to have her spin straw on the third night, she disappeared without a trace."

Disappeared without a trace...

The words chilled the Woodcutter. Rapunzel, too, had been abducted, and her appearance in the Wood came dangerously close to having deadly consequences. He had to get back to the Wood. Maid Maleen's life might depend upon it.

The Duke leaned against the wall, his energy spent from recounting the events. "It was only after all this transpired that I learned of my advisor's betrayal and greed."

The Duke sat down in his chair and buried his face in his hands. "It is my fault, and I must find her. I must find where she disappeared to. If anything happened to her..."

The Woodcutter pounded him bracingly upon the back. "Trouble no more maidens in your duchy. I shall return her to you."

The Duke nodded, but the Woodcutter could see that the Duke did not believe him.

CHAPTER 30

The Woodcutter stretched his feet toward the flames in the hearth. After their talk of Maid Maleen, he and the Duke had spoken at length about the magic that was appearing in the Duchy of Plainness. The Duke had made it clear that he did not care for the power of the fae; he only cared for the girl who had once wielded it.

The Woodcutter believed him.

He hoped that finding Maid Maleen would chase the magic from the land and stop the snowfalls, much as Rapunzel's union with her true love calmed the wildness and set the path straight. It was a strange thing, the warm snows...

If true love could not conquer the draw of the snows to the duchy, if the magic still fell from the sky, the duchy would join the Twelve Kingdoms. The Ruler of Ordinary had been clear that magic was unwanted in his borders.

But the Ruler would not be pleased having land annexed to the fae.

The innkeeper brought the Woodcutter an earthen cup filled with tea, which he took gratefully. Her redheaded daughter, with her twisted limbs, played quietly with a kitten, dragging a bit of straw across the floor and laughing thickly as the kitten stalked it.

The fragrance of the tea filled the Woodcutter's nose.

It was a familiar smell—black leaves and elderberry.

He could almost feel his wife's hand upon his shoulder, her gentle touch resting on the back of his neck. He closed his eyes and allowed the warmth and the darkness to lull him to sleep.

He opened his eyes to the dim glow of the dying embers.

The crippled, red-haired girl was standing over him with a knife made of elk bone, poised to plunge it into his heart.

She whispered, "Please stop me."

And then the blade flashed downward.

CHAPTER 31

The Woodcutter turned quickly to the right, and the bone cut his upper arm. He cried out in pain. The girl ripped the jagged shard from his body and readied herself to bring it down again. He knew she would not miss this time.

But her eyes.

There was such pleading in her eyes.

"Please," she begged.

He fell to the ground, and the knife penetrated his chair. He watched as she fought her very own hands, watched as her hands tried to rip the knife from the cushioned back.

He tried to stand, but the room kept swimming.

She was focused solely upon the blade. Her hands bled blue, cut upon the edge of the knife as she fought herself. "Please run. Please. I cannot hold much longer."

The Woodcutter stumbled behind her and pinned her arms to her sides. He held her as she sobbed, as she strained toward the knife. He held her as she screamed with rage.

The door opened.

The innkeeper pounded out of the other room, a mother grizzly protecting her cub.

"What are you doing to my child?" she roared.

The Woodcutter shouted as he struggled with her daughter, "She is bewitched."

The mother grabbed onto the Woodcutter's arm and dug her sharp nails into his wound.

He cried out as he let go of the redheaded girl. The child dashed to the knife. This time she was able to free it. She turned and raised it to bring it down again.

The Woodcutter grabbed the girl up again as the mother shrank back in fear.

"What have you done to her?" she wept.

"The blade!" he shouted. "Free her of the blade!"

And then the young girl screamed, "Believe him!"

The mother grabbed a broom from the corner. As she got closer to her daughter, the young girl lunged. The mother pulled back, but the girl screamed at her, "Help me!"

This time her mother did not hesitate.

She struck her daughter's wrist with such force the knife flew across the room and landed upon the floor.

And then the knife began to draw back toward the girl.

The girl's right hand hung broken, but her left hand reached.

"Help me!" she cried.

The mother tried to grab the knife, but it spun away and scurried faster toward the girl.

"Mother!"

And then the Woodcutter felt something stir within his jacket.

Something wriggled and forced its way out. The pixie, injured and unwell, flew weakly into the air. It eyed the dancing blade, and the blade slowed its progress, almost warily.

Skittering across the floor, the knife circled the fae, and then the two magical beings threw themselves at one another.

The blade twitched as it rose into the air, and blue blood fell from the faerie.

But the pixie held on.

It held on as the knife bit into it. It held on as its blood wept from the tip. It held on until the blade stopped jerking, and the redheaded girl stilled and the wildness left her eyes.

Finally the pixie let the blade drop. The knife clanged upon the floor and remained motionless.

The pixie hovered as the Woodcutter released the girl and she slumped to the floor.

The pixie looked at the Woodcutter.

And the Woodcutter knew.

He knew.

The pixie's eyes became dark as night and they began to close.

The pixie fell so quietly as the whole world screamed.

The Woodcutter ran, dodging the innkeeper, who rushed to her daughter's side, whose red blood could not hear the pixie's fall toward the earth.

The Woodcutter ran and he held out his hand.

He held out his hand, and as the pixie dropped, the Wood-cutter felt time stop.

And then.

He felt the pixie, felt it heavy upon his palm, heavy with the sadness of the whole world, bleeding blue blood upon his hand.

The Woodcutter turned to the innkeeper. "I need your tree."

She shook her head. "We have no trees here."

He felt the pixie fading.

It was beyond his power.

"Do you have any dust?"

She shook her head. "We don't use such…" Her eyes shifted nervously with the lies that would rather destroy than admit the truth of her shame.

"Your dust," he demanded. "It's dying…"

The mother looked at the pixie and looked at the Woodcutter.

She was silent as she struggled. Silent as she fought truth with pride, as the forces waged battle within her head.

"In the back of the cupboard."

The Woodcutter ran as if the pixie's wings were attached to his feet. He ripped open the cupboard, and there in the back was a small tin.

He fumbled with the cover, his fingers slippery with the blue blood, but he was able to open the tin. He bathed the pixie in the sparkling powder.

The faerie's light pulsed, slow as a sleeping heartbeat.

Pulsing.

Pulsing.

The pixie opened its eyes and swallowed.

Its small mouth gasped.

The light did not fade, but the pixie just barely shone and all the dust was gone.

The mother sat, her daughter cradled within her arms. She rocked back and forth as she begged, "Forgive me…forgive me…I did not mean…"

The Woodcutter stared at her, the pieces fitting together.

The Woodcutter took the pixie and placed it upon her daughter's heart. The pixie snuggled within the divot of the girl's neck, the nook in between her clavicles where the pulse of her heart gently beat.

"What are you doing to her?" the mother gasped.

The pixie's glow began to beat in rhythm to the girl's heart.

The Woodcutter said nothing and just smoothed the girl's red hair.

Her legs were the first to straighten. They stretched out like caterpillars and smoothed out her clawed feet. Her back uncurled.

As the pixie's light became brighter, the girl's neck aligned, holding her head tall. The blue blood upon her hands turned red.

Iron was everywhere in this land, ingested in the food, ingested in the water. The girl stooped because the iron in her body fought with the dust, fought with her blood as it ran artificially blue.

The Woodcutter looked at the mother, understanding to what length she had gone to have her child spin gold from straw, to what length she had gone to make a duchess of her child.

To what length she had hungered for the power of the fae.

She had fed her own child dust.

The mother's eyes were full of tears. "Please, don't tell anyone. I promise...I just wanted her to have a better life..."

But the words rang hollow.

The Woodcutter took the tiny pixie and tucked it gently within his breast pocket.

He turned to the mother as she held her daughter tight, and he whispered, "No more."

But he knew she did not understand.

CHAPTER 32

The stalk rose high up into the air. So high, its top disappeared into the clouds.

The Woodcutter stood at the base, shielding his eyes with his hands.

The farm was quiet. A few chickens scratched in the yard. A skinny cat slept in the dust.

"That brat came home swearing they were magic beans. I'll be damned."

A cagey woman had come up behind him. She was so close he could smell her rotting teeth. "All I can say is that this thing had better start blooming. I don't have time to take care of something that don't give back."

She shuffled up to the fifteen-foot-wide plant and stingily watered it with her little can.

The stalk responded by unfurling a leaf sixty feet above the Woodcutter's head.

The woman shook her fist. "Is that the best you can do? We were better off with that fool cow!"

She shuffled back to the house, scattering the hungry chickens in her path.

The Woodcutter stood for a moment, contemplating the stalk.

He then placed his hand upon its body and began to climb.

CHAPTER 33

The clouds were solid.

They should not have been.

The Woodcutter stepped tentatively onto the hardened mist and was disturbed that it held his weight. He reached down and broke off a piece, lifting it to his nose. He dropped it like a burning coal.

Dust.

Vaporized dust held in the atmosphere, a massive storage shed in the sky.

The Woodcutter swayed as the rush of free magic coursed through his veins. A sense of well-being and a desire to lie down and rest his weary eyes overwhelmed him. The sky seemed bluer and the sun friendly. The light fractured into rainbows that hid in the nooks and crevasses of the fluffy goodness.

He retched and he bent over to vomit.

His eyes blurred, but he caught the shape of a gray stone path bisecting the clouds. He forced himself to stumble toward them.

His feet hit the stones and the disorientation lifted. His hands shook as he held them up. He clenched and unclenched his fingers. Still they shook.

The dust was powerful.

He looked around. The dust clouds stretched for miles before touching the solid land found in the Kingdom of the Clouds.

The harvest...

The number of pixies that had been destroyed to gather such dust...

He bent over to vomit again.

As he stood, the pixie tugged at his pocket. He reached in and carefully brought the blinking creature out into the light. The fae's pupils constricted and dilated to the rhythm of the heart he could feel beating within its breast, but then it fixated upon the Woodcutter and held out its hand toward his temple.

He could feel the power transfer, could feel as the last of the dust left him. The pixie's throbbing glow steadied for just a moment as it absorbed the magic.

The Woodcutter looked at the clouds that surrounded them. Careful to keep his feet upon the path, the Woodcutter lowered the faerie to the dust.

The pixie's eyes became clear and it seemed to wake. The cloud began to shift. It seemed to be drawn to the faerie like smoke to an open window.

The Woodcutter could feel the transfer of wild magic to the creature of air. The pixie began to levitate, its strength returning.

And then the Woodcutter heard an awful roar.

"Fee, fi, fo, fum..."

The words rumbled low and dangerously. The path began to shake. The Woodcutter looked over his shoulder to see the head of a giant crest over a cumulus formation.

He looked back at the pixie and whispered, "Faster, little one."

It jerked slightly, like a hiccup. Then it jerked again and was out of his hands. It flipped in the air in joy and tore through the cloud, absorbing the dust as it flew, leaving a hole that looked down upon the boggy farmland below.

"Who steals from my crop?"

The monster was drawing closer.

The Woodcutter looked for a place to hide, but the fields of dust would kill him. So he stood still, hoping the Giant was near-sighted and would pass.

But he didn't.

He fixed the Woodcutter with a terrible gaze.

"I smell a tree."

The Woodcutter shrugged.

The Giant swept out a terrible paw and picked up the Wood-cutter. "My fire needs fuel, and you shall do just fine."

CHAPTER 34

The kitchen stretched as far as the eye could see.

A woman with a shelf-like rump the size of two large pigs stood stirring a boiling cauldron. Her hair was pulled back beneath a dust rag. Her peasant smock covered her boulder-like bosoms. She turned, yellow teeth snarling, "What took you so long?"

The Giant threw the Woodcutter and a few tree trunks into the wood box.

"A mousy-like tree that was eatin' at my clouds."

The Giantess fixed the Woodcutter with her one good eye. "A little mousy tree?"

"Smells like a tree. Eats like a mouse. Figure it's a new breed."

She let out a wheezing, hacking laugh. "A new breed of tree? You're a fool."

She turned around and hit the Giant over the head with her wooden spoon. "He's no such thing. He's a twig of wood that got too close to that dust of yours. Now if you'll set the table, I'll finish getting supper ready."

The Giant heaved a heavy sigh and turned to take the large saucers from the shelf.

The Woodcutter sat himself down upon a log as the Giant and his wife settled into dinner.

An uneasy silence fell upon the two as they slurped down their soup.

"Did you see the old Crone today?"

The Giant grunted. "I mwenft—"

"Don't talk with your mouth full. I said, did you see the Crone today? That dust field of yours is blowing into my petunias, and I swear to goodness, one of them bit my ankle and now it's all swollen up."

The Giant put down his bread and swallowed.

The Woodcutter leaned forward.

"I did just as you said. Over the hill. Into the woods. Left at the great tree. But I didn't find no Crone."

The Giantess threw her bread at his head. "You old fool. Over the hill?"

"Yes."

"Into the woods?"

"Yes."

"Left at the great tree?"

"Yes."

"Well, you did something wrong."

"I didn't do nuthin' wrong."

"I swear to goodness, a body has to do everything herself around here. You worthless piece of..."

"Now don't you go sayin' anything ugly."

"Are you calling me ugly?"

"Now that isn't what I said..."

"I think you just did. I was sitting right here and I heard you."

The Woodcutter carved the instructions into a scrap of bark and placed it in his pocket, but leapt to his feet at the Giant's cry, "Fee! Fi! Fo! Fum! I smell the blood of a human!"

The Giantess whacked him in the side of the arm. "Sit down, you old fool. That's just the roast."

The Giant sat, but his eyes wandered around the kitchen.

"If you're going to sit there jumping out of your skin, you can do it in the other room. This attitude of yours is souring my stomach."

The Giant threw down his spoon. "Woman, I give you a good life."

The Giantess threw down her spoon. "You give me no such thing."

"Look at this house."

"We live in a rat hole."

"Look at your garden."

"Weedy mess."

"What more do you want?" he roared.

"You are a stingy old bastard, and I should have listened to my father."

The Giant stood, knocking over his chair.

The Woodcutter's eyes caught a flash of brown hair ducking behind a broom in the corner.

"My father was twice the man you'll ever be!" said the Giantess.

The Giant walked over to the cupboard and threw open the door. "If it weren't for me working my fingers to the bone to farm these dust fields for that Queen, we'd be living in the woods like that Crone." He grabbed a heavy, jangling sack and threw it upon the table. Gold coins the size of watermelons spilled upon the floor. "Here. Take it. Take it all. If that will make you shut your claptrap for one blessed moment…"

"Claptrap? CLAPTRAP!"

Her eyes never left the Giant as she grabbed the broom from the corner, revealing the hiding place of a scrawny human boy with chestnut-colored curls. His face, down to his very freckles, drained of color as he stood, frozen in fear.

The Woodcutter, ever keeping an eye on the fighting couple, motioned for the boy to run to the woodpile.

The Giantess began raining blows upon the Giant's head. "Don't you darken my doorway again!"

"Your doorway? I built this house with my own two hands, woman!"

The Giant began throwing cups and saucers. Huge fragments rained down upon the ground as the Giantess broke them with her broom handle as fast as the Giant could hurl.

The boy dodged the debris as he ran toward the woodpile. He crouched beside the Woodcutter, shaking in fright.

A faint niggling sensation itched at the back of the Woodcutter.

The Woodcutter set down his pack.

His hands rested for a moment and then pulled out the gift of the peddler.

Carefully, he unwrapped it.

A harp.

It was a golden harp with a woman trapped upon the pillar. She looked at him, eyes full of trust and pleading.

The Woodcutter sat the harp upon his lap. He laid his fingers upon the strings.

And then plucked.

The voice of the woman of the harp rang out in accompaniment to the music.

At once, the Giant and Giantess stopped.

Their arms lowered and their eyes glazed over.

Their knees became weak, and soon they were upon the floor, snoring like bears.

The Woodcutter stopped playing and the Giants began to stir.

He placed his fingers upon the harp once more. He turned to the young boy and whispered, "What's your name?"

The boy swallowed hard. "Jack."

The Woodcutter smiled at the frightened boy. "Well, Jack, I am afraid that this beanstalk is my fault. I gave some beans to a peddler, and I believe he sold them to you."

Jack nodded.

"It seems that, as long as someone plays this instrument, the harp will sing them to sleep. Do you know how to play the harp, Jack?" the Woodcutter asked.

Jack shook his head no. He was trying so hard to be brave.

The Woodcutter transferred the harp to Jack's lap. "Well, Jack, now seems just as good a time as any for you to learn."

Jack's fingers were hard and discordant upon the strings, and the woman's voice changed.

The Giants began to stir once more.

The Woodcutter could see the young boy begin to panic.

He took Jack's hand in his. "Gentle, son. Gentle."

Son.

The Woodcutter caught himself.

Jack's fingers strummed more quietly, and the Giants settled back into snoring.

The Woodcutter turned to the lady of the harp. "Milady, this boy here has never had the pleasure of meeting one such as yourself. I would ask that you help him to keep the music sweet."

She nodded, her voice not changing her tune.

The Woodcutter turned to Jack. "I have to leave."

A horrible note came from the harp.

The Giants snorted before rolling over.

"But I will be back. You must play until I return. You must play no matter what. There is only so long that the Giant will believe your smell is just the pot roast. You know that, don't you?"

Jack nodded seriously.

"I will not be long."

The Woodcutter dashed across the floor and out to the path as fast as his legs would carry him.

CHAPTER 35

The Woodcutter had walked over the hill and into the woods and had taken a left at the great tree. He walked into the clearing. Settled into the earth was a round-bottomed fortress with many chimneys and windows but no door. A fence of human bones marked the border of the yard from the forest.

He had not understood when Oberon and Titania had told him to seek the Crone. He had not understood that they meant *the* Crone. If he had known, he wondered if he would have come. But he was there, so the Woodcutter opened the gate and walked in.

He looked up at the blank wall of the fortress. His power in the Kingdom of the Clouds was less than that in the Twelve Kingdoms, but he opened his mouth and commanded, "Turn your back to the forest, your front to me."

The fortress creaked and groaned, and slowly it spun until the back was to the front and the front was to the back, and before the Woodcutter was a door.

The Woodcutter stepped forward to knock, noting the gnashing teeth in the keyhole, but turned quickly as a crashing sound tore through the trees.

Riding upon a stone mortar the size of a grown man was a lovely woman with dark-black hair. The mortar sailed upon the ground like a ship on the ocean, directed by a pestle the woman used as a rudder. The mortar flew into the front yard and the maiden leapt off, as graceful as an acrobat. She regarded the Woodcutter sharply as the mortar put itself away behind the fortress. She sniffed the air. "You are a man, yet smell of a tree. That means you can be only one being. Good afternoon, Woodcutter."

The woman was young, but she could not deceive the Woodcutter's eye.

The Woodcutter bowed. "Baba Yaga."

The maiden laid her finger on the side of her nose. "What brings you so far into the Kingdom of the Clouds?"

"I have been told to seek the Crone."

Even as he said it, her shape began sagging, turning from young to old. Baba Yaga sighed as her breasts dropped and her waist expanded.

"They said this Kingdom in the Clouds was full of blue roses, a supply large enough to make tea to keep my youth forever. I am afraid they lied." She looked at the Woodcutter. "But the memory of the Maiden is still fresh. You are lucky. You shall reap the benefits of the Maiden's kindness, but also the wisdom of the Crone."

Baba Yaga walked to her house. The teeth in the keyhole quieted themselves as the door swung open. Unbidden, the Woodcutter followed her in. With each step, the woman aged, adding a wrinkle to her face.

The Woodcutter felt invisible hands upon his arm, removing his heavy pack from his back. He thanked the invisible servant. The bone fence was made of those heroes who had not minded their manners. Baba Yaga was no mere faerie. She was the Dark Lady, the Wild One. With a tea made of blue roses, she was the Maiden, kind and loving. As the Crone, she was a formidable enemy.

Indeed, the Woodcutter was lucky he had found her when he did.

Baba Yaga flung herself into a crude rocker, the Crone taking over, and snapped at him, "Well, why are you here, then? Why have you come to bother me?"

"A question, Baba Yaga."

She nodded toward a chair, indicating the Woodcutter was allowed to sit. Two bowls of stew floated through the air and landed upon two small trays set up beside the chairs.

The stew was green and smelled of dead things. Baba Yaga took the bowl and began shoveling the foul concoction into her mouth. She motioned to the Woodcutter to eat, eyeing him as he lifted the spoon to his mouth.

The stew was slime and rot. The Woodcutter smiled as he swallowed.

Baba Yaga cackled. "You're a strong one, Woodcutter, to eat the meal presented by the Dark Lady. You are so polite to your host. Such a shame. I would have used you as my Yule log come the heart of winter."

The Woodcutter picked up his spoon and ate another bite, smacking his lips appreciatively.

Baba Yaga pounded upon her knee. "Indeed, you have earned yourself a question."

She pulled a pipe from her apron and struggled to light it, her clawed fingers fumbling. Baba Yaga puffed, hacking and coughing a bit before settling in. "Well, what do you want? State your question."

"King Oberon and Queen Titania sent me."

Baba Yaga smiled. "Old Oberon and Titania sent you? My, I haven't talked to them in years. We used to ride the Midsummer's Eve together." She chuckled softly. "Once, we asked Odin if he had ever hunted snipe."

"They said you would know how to stop a hellhound who no longer responds to Odin's call."

Baba Yaga stopped rocking and looked at the Platinum Ax that hung from the Woodcutter's side. "Terrible times they are.

Terrible times if a Woodcutter has to get an Ax from a River God." She peered forward, shaking her pipe at him. "You're lucky you didn't lose your father's ax getting that thing. You didn't lose it, did you? You show it to me. Show me it is fine."

The Woodcutter took his father's ax from his other side. Baba Yaga reached out and touched it fondly with one finger. "My, I never thought I would see this again. Your great-great-great-grandfather was a good man, and never you forget it. He could eat the entire bowl of my stew."

She leaned back, taking another puff of her pipe and hacking some more before closing her eyes. "That I should see the day that a hellhound won't come to his master…that a Woodcutter should be forced to round up a puppy…"

She opened her eyes and pointed at the Woodcutter. "There's a way, but are you willing?"

The Woodcutter did not hesitate. "I would not be here otherwise."

She leaned forward, staring at him dead in the eye. "Why? Why are you so concerned about Odin losing one of his mutts?"

He did not blink as he replied. "Have you ever heard a pixie touch the ground?"

Her face drained of all color until it was as white as the pale moon. "Indeed."

The Woodcutter left Baba Yaga's castle wiser, but more frightened than he had ever been before in his life.

CHAPTER 36

The Woodcutter crept back into the house. The Giants slept as he dashed to the woodpile.

Jack played on. Blood ran down his soft fingers. The strings of the harp wept red.

The Woodcutter's heart felt cut to the quick.

He took the harp from Jack's hand quickly, without stopping the song. "I shall play while you escape. You must run. You must run as fast as you can to the stalk and return home."

Jack stood, unsure. "What about you?"

"Go, child," said the Woodcutter.

Big tears filled his eyes. "My mother…"

The Woodcutter understood.

He had met Jack's mother.

"Take the coins the Giant threw. You must hurry."

Jack tucked a giant coin beneath each arm and scurried toward the door. But he paused, looking back for just a moment. Then he ran—ran hard and ran fast until he was out of sight.

Then the Woodcutter placed his hands upon the harp's strings and silenced her music.

CHAPTER 37

The Giants woke and stretched.

"Must've nodded off," said the Giant. "What were you saying?"

"You never listen to me," spat his wife.

The Giant stood and strode over to the wood box. The Woodcutter was busy tucking the harp safely in his sack and did not see the Giant as he reached in and grabbed the Woodcutter and several other tree trunks to feed to the fire.

The Giantess swayed and grumbled at her husband, "I'm going to take a nap. You bore me."

The Giant threw another tree into the hearth.

The Woodcutter heard the Giantess's booming steps as she climbed the stairs to her room.

The Woodcutter struggled to free himself from the Giant, but his arms were pinned at his sides and unable to reach his Ax.

The Giant threw another tree in the flames, lost in thought. The Woodcutter opened his mouth and said, "You are correct, you know."

The Giant stopped. "Did you say something?" He brought his face close.

"Indeed. I am a new breed of tree."

The Giant gave the Woodcutter a shake and then turned him this way and that. "You smell like a regular piece of wood. In you go."

"Wait! I speak the truth! I am a rare specimen. Quite rare. I grow only the most magical fruit."

The Giant eyed him once again. "Magical fruit?"

"Indeed, I have grown you a harp."

The Giant eyed him suspiciously. "A harp? Harps don't grow on trees."

"Where do they come from, then?"

The Giant stopped, stumped for an answer. "Well, I don't know. But I know they sure as heck don't grow on trees."

"But you see, I am a magic tree."

"A magic tree?"

"A magic tree that grows harps."

The Giant freed the Woodcutter just enough that he could reach into his pack and pull out the lady.

The Giant smiled. "Well, lookie here. I got me a magic tree. Now give me my new harp."

The Woodcutter felt the lady tremble in his arms. "Oh, but you see, she is not quite ripe yet. You should plant me in the ground."

"I want the harp ripe—now."

"But she is not fully grown. You will have nothing but a plain harp if you take her, but if you give her a week to grow, you shall have a magic talking harp who can tell the future."

"You don't say…"

"I do."

The Giant stroked his whiskery chin. "All right, then, sproutling. You grow me this magical harp and we'll see what's what."

The Giant gave the Woodcutter a little shake. "But you better be a tree and not a twig trying to fool us."

The Woodcutter sagely replied, "I am definitely not a twig."

The garden was lovely, rich with flowers the size of a toddler. The Woodcutter waited, planted in the dirt to his knees, for night to fall. The Giant came out every hour to sprinkle water upon the Woodcutter's head and to see if the harp had grown any larger.

The Woodcutter leaned against the harp, his eyes lulling closed in the growing heat of the day, when he was startled by the rustle of a golden-leafed bush. The harp gasped.

A small, dirty face looked out at him.

"Jack, what are you doing here?" the Woodcutter asked.

"I couldn't leave you. I couldn't leave you with that monster."

The Woodcutter's face broke into a rare smile. "Now, Jack, I am fine."

Jack's voice seemed highly distressed. "But you're buried to your knees in the dirt."

"Merely waiting for darkness to fall and the giants to go to sleep."

Jack's face fell, flushed red in embarrassment.

The Woodcutter reached out as best he could. "Jack, you have a very courageous heart, but you must hurry. The Giant will be here soon to water me."

At that moment, the earth began to rumble.

"Fee! Fi! Fo! Fum! I smell the blood of a human!"

Jack froze, his eyes wide in fright.

"My escape, fortunately, has come sooner than expected," said the Woodcutter. He leaned forward to Jack and whispered in a low voice, "You must run as fast as you can to the beanstalk. I shall distract the Giant. When you get to the base, you must begin cutting down the stalk."

"But what about you?"

The Woodcutter patted Jack's head. His hands paused upon the sandy curls as a protective surge for this child welled up strangely inside.

"Son..."

The word slipped from his lips without thinking.

Son.

The Giant tore out a rutabaga and heaved it into the air, sending it dangerously close.

"I shall be fine," the Woodcutter said. "Now go."

Jack nodded and took off.

The Woodcutter freed his legs from the soil and turned to the harp. "Are you ready to help save both our lives?"

The Giant stopped as he heard the harp cry, "Giant! Oh, Giant! Someone steals your harp! Help me, oh, Giant!"

"HUMAN!" the Giant roared.

The Woodcutter began running, the harp shouting in his arms. Into the woods he ran, leading the Giant away from the child he had accidentally called "son."

The Woodcutter hid behind a tree.

The lady of the harp smothered a giggle as the Giant clomped nearby, overthrowing rocks and moss-covered logs.

As the Giant plowed through a brook and continued farther into the forest, the Woodcutter whispered to the lady, "I believe we are safe."

He lifted the harp and began running in the opposite direction, but just as they reached the tree line, the Woodcutter's foot caught on a rock. He stumbled forward, causing the harp's strings to vibrate. She held her hands over her mouth, as if to silence the noise.

But in the distance, the Woodcutter heard the Giant bellow, "HUMAN! I've got you now!"

The Woodcutter ran.

He ran past the Giant's house and down the path through the dust fields. The Woodcutter could feel the Giant's thundering steps shake the stones beneath his feet. The Giant was still far behind, but gaining.

The Woodcutter tucked the harp into his sack. She smiled at him as she disappeared beneath the flap. He swung himself onto the stalk and started to descend.

Halfway down, the beanstalk swayed violently. The Woodcutter looked up and saw the Giant had reached the top of the plant.

The Woodcutter sped to the base.

As the Woodcutter's feet hit the ground, he turned to Jack, who stood with an ax hanging limply in his scabbed fingers. The wounds from playing the harp had reopened and tears were in the child's eyes. He looked pitifully at the Woodcutter, as if apologizing for his inability to make anything more than a small dent.

The Woodcutter placed his hand upon the stalk, feeling it tremble as it supported the Giant's weight. "Gentle stalk, I ask you to sacrifice your life for the life of this boy."

The stalk sighed sadly and then whispered, *Yes.*

The Woodcutter ripped the ax from Jack's limp hand and began hacking furiously.

The stalk helped, ripping itself at its base.

The Woodcutter was halfway through when the stalk seemed to transform from plant to rock hardness. The blow of his ax rang harshly through his body. The stalk whispered urgently, *Hush!*

The Woodcutter looked. He reached out his senses. He tried to find what caused the stalk to give a warning.

There was no magic…

But then he looked up, and then he saw.

As the stalk swayed, it dashed its uppermost limbs upon the vaporized magic, which now began to fall like snow upon the Farm of Ordinariness.

"No…no…" the Woodcutter whispered.

He placed his hands upon the stalk, as if they could repair the damage done.

But the stalk had been cut too far.

As the Giant fell, he brought down half the sky.

Brought down the sky of dust.

The Woodcutter grabbed Jack by the wrist and raced him beneath a fragile lean-to that stood next to the pigpens of Jack's home. The Woodcutter hid the boy beneath his coat as he watched. He could feel the child tremble.

With the mortal thud of the Giant touching the earth, Jack's mother stepped from her home.

"Go inside!" the Woodcutter shouted.

"Who do you think you are, you lousy, stinking—" she shouted back.

She was cut off mid-insult as the dust fell upon her skin.

She looked up at the sky and touched the flake. She shook her fist. "Whaddya mean by this? Warm snow?"

Her eyes glazed over and her jaw went slack as half the sky fell upon her.

"Mother!" Jack cried. He pulled away the Woodcutter's jacket and struggled toward her.

"Stop! You must not run!" the Woodcutter said, holding Jack back and out of the dust.

He knew, even as Jack wiggled in his arms.

He knew as the darkness overtook the day and chased away the light.

He knew as Jack's mother stood, glowing in the shower of faerie dust, more dust than any red-blooded human should have ever come in contact with, as the land was bathed in more dust than any iron could repel.

He knew what was coming next.

He watched powerlessly as the normal land was transformed to magic, as the farm was transformed to a Kingdom, and as the plain farmer was transformed to a blue blood and a queen whose heart was wild and unclaimed.

The wind whipped wildly and lightning cracked.

The magic called out like a lantern on the dark sea.

He heard the Beast.

He heard the footfalls. He heard the snarls.

He looked over to the Queen of this new Thirteenth Kingdom, and he saw that she heard it, too.

And she began to run.

The Woodcutter shielded Jack's eyes.

He could do nothing, not without risking Jack.

He could not risk another child's life...

Small hands next to the flowers on the floor...

He could do nothing to save the woman.

Glass slippers upon the tiny blue-veined feet.

His breath caught in his throat.

He felt Jack tremble.

He watched as the Beast was upon the child's mother.

Watched as her body dropped to the ground.

"Mother!" Jack cried.

The Woodcutter felt her soul disappear.

The darkness lifted from the Thirteenth Kingdom and all was still.

Jack struggled, and this time the Woodcutter did not hold him back.

"Mother..." Jack's tears spilled from his eyes as he bent over the woman.

The Woodcutter was sure his heart would break.

Just then the earth shimmered.

And the Woodcutter saw a House he had hoped to never see again.

"Come, Jack," he spoke. "We must leave now."

He grasped the boy by the hand and turned.

And found himself in the ballroom of the Gentleman.

CHAPTER 38

The Gentleman looked as sickly as ever in the pale, washed-out light of the ballroom.

"Well, well, Woodcutter." The Gentleman stood from his dais and slunk to their side. "It seems you have more a taste for dust than you let on."

The Woodcutter's eyes hardened. "Let us go."

The Gentleman laughed. "But you see, you are now in my Kingdom, a Kingdom recently appointed to me as the only blue blood in the area."

The Woodcutter gripped Jack closely, his hand itching to unleash the Platinum Ax.

But there was only one Ax from the River God left, one Ax to use against the hellhound.

The Woodcutter stilled his anger.

The Gentleman was amused. "You fascinate me so, Wood-cutter. You cost me a great deal in our last visit and continue to cost me a great deal. That little stunt with the dust fields, although nice enough to annex this farm, has set me back. And so I'm afraid that I must insist on you remaining my guest for quite a bit longer."

"We have played this game before," the Woodcutter said coldly.

"Tsk, tsk, Woodcutter. You have so little imagination. I'm afraid you haven't played this particular game."

The Gentleman walked up to Jack. The Woodcutter stepped between the Gentleman and the child.

"Now, little boy, I bet you would like a treat," said the Gentleman.

Jack peeked around the Woodcutter's coat, his voice full of tears. "I just want my mother."

The Gentleman leered. "And you shall have your mother."

The Gentleman removed a silver snuffbox from his coat pocket. With a wink, he opened it slowly.

The Woodcutter forced the boy behind him.

But he heard a female's laugh to the right. And to the left. And behind. The Woodcutter spun. They were surrounded by the revelers, each holding a silver box to her lips. The Woodcutter's hand unstrapped the Platinum Ax.

The revelers blew, and the shimmering white powder settled in Jack's eyes.

The Gentleman clapped his hand and the ballroom was night.

The revelers laughed drunkenly and paired up, dancing away.

The Woodcutter held tight to Jack, but the world seemed to stop as an elegant woman dressed in scarlet stepped forward. On her cheek was the beauty patch shaped as a flower.

Jack pulled away and ran to the woman, shouting, "Mother!"

She scooped him up into her arms and gave the Woodcutter a sly smile as she held the boy close to her heaving breast.

The Woodcutter stepped forward, but when Jack saw him, he screamed, "Mother! Run!"

The woman turned her back, and Jack blubbered, "Mother, I thought that wolf was going to eat you…"

He said "that wolf" as he stared in fear at the Woodcutter.

The Gentleman ran his finger along the rim of his goblet in delight as he stepped closer to the Woodcutter. "So, you see, you are free to go. But I'm afraid…Oh, what was his name?"

The lady in scarlet caught the question and asked the small boy, "Show me what a bright boy you are. Spell your name for Mummy."

Jack giggled. "I don't know how."

"Well, you say your name, and I shall spell it for you."

"Jack, silly Mother…"

"J-A-C-K," she said, tweaking his nose.

The Gentleman turned back to the Woodcutter. "As I was saying, Jack doesn't seem to want to leave."

"Jack, come here!" the Woodcutter commanded.

Jack's face grew pale and his eyes were as wide as silver dollars as he clung to the woman's skirts. "Mother, the wolf! I can hear its cry!"

The Woodcutter reached his senses down to the earth and started to weave the spell to break the illusion.

The magic cut off midstream. It snapped back at the Woodcutter like a stroke from a wooden switch.

The Gentleman wagged his finger. "Now, now, Woodcutter. I don't allow that here. All magic must stay in the house."

The Woodcutter clenched his jaw.

"Like I said, you are free to go, but I'm afraid Jack seems to want to stay."

The woman had taken Jack by the hand and was leading him away. "Now, dear, you must be hungry. Let's go get you a snack."

"Little boys are such imaginative creatures." The Gentleman smiled.

"What do you want?" demanded the Woodcutter.

"To keep you out of my way," the Gentleman snarled.

Jack was surrounded by a group of giggling ladies. The woman in scarlet mimed a dish and passed it to the child. Jack took it with such excitement and ate the air, declaring it the best food he had ever tasted. The ladies laughed in delight.

The Woodcutter bowed his head. He would stay until the child was safe. He would wait for Jack.

The Woodcutter sat in the darkened window, his pipe creating wreaths of smoke around his head. Jack slept upon the billowing gown of a nameless female. His sweaty hair was plastered to his forehead, and he tossed fitfully. Dark circles were already beneath his eyes, and shadows clung to the child's face. There was too much dust in the House for a young, red-blooded boy.

The Woodcutter knew a way to get them both out, but there was a risk and he did not want to risk Jack. Not Jack. Not the child he had accidentally called "son."

He knew he had been brought to the Vanishing House for a reason. Fate was not so cruel to twice allow such a chance encounter. The House held the answers to the mysteries he had been charged to solve.

Even so, the Gentleman would pay for holding them prisoner.

The red-dressed woman with the beauty patch sat down beside him. "You rudely ended our conversation last time we spoke."

There was enchantment around her. Not dizzy with the dust, he could sense it now. The Woodcutter said nothing, but continued to puff on his pipe.

She pouted, running a long red nail beneath his lapel. "Even little Jack wasn't able to give me your name. Nothing besides 'Woodcutter.'"

The enchantment tried to weave around his head like a lover's caress.

She whispered in his ear, "But perhaps we could help one another."

The Woodcutter continued to look straight ahead.

"Don't fret. I am not asking for your name—just a trade. A little information and you shall receive that which you hold so dear. I am looking for a stepdaughter of mine. She has skin as white as snow and hair as black as ebony. I'm sure you remember her. My huntsman died while trying to protect her there in your Wood. But we couldn't find any trace of my little one, and I am so worried."

She brought her face dangerously close. The Woodcutter could smell the cloves upon her breath.

"You tell me where to find my stepdaughter, and I shall bring you Jack."

The Woodcutter exhaled a plume of smoke. It struck at the enchantment like a snake, choking it as a constrictor does its prey.

She got up, coughing. And then she laughed. She leaned into him, amused. "Remember my offer."

He stared up into the ring of clean smoke as she walked away.

She was searching for her stepdaughter.

His eyes drifted to her lazily across the crowd and fixed upon the back of her neck. The woman in scarlet red shifted her weight as she laughed.

He knew who she was.

She was the second wife of the King of the Sixth Kingdom, married shortly after the first wife had died in childbirth. This woman in scarlet with the flower-shaped beauty mark was Snow White's stepmother. She was the Queen.

CHAPTER 39

The Woodcutter rose and stretched. He felt the Queen's eyes upon him as he walked to the doorway. He did not like to leave Jack, but with the Queen in the House, he was almost sure this was the place Snow White and the Peddler had spoken of; this was the place where the pixies were being destroyed. He had made a promise to the Mother Dryad. He did not know how to both help Jack and free the pixies, but life had taught him to place one foot before the other and the answer would come when it was time.

The moment he exited the ballroom and went into the hallway, the light returned to normal. Morning was breaking.

The Gentleman followed him out and lounged against the door frame. "Going so soon?" he asked.

The Woodcutter walked around the foyer, examining the art upon the wall. It had not been there before. The House had shifted since he had met it in the Wood. The hallway had been eaten by a swooping staircase. He had hoped to trace the path of Snow White to the hidden workroom she had spoken of, but now only two doorways were on the main floor. One led to the ballroom. The other exited the House.

The Gentleman gave the Woodcutter a sly smile. "So, you know, you will probably not find us again if you step out the front door for a breath of fresh air. This House has a habit of moving."

"I shall keep that in mind," answered the Woodcutter.

The Gentleman winked and returned to the ballroom.

The Woodcutter waited until the door closed, and then he climbed the stairs to the second floor.

The first room was a large bedroom with a window that looked out upon a battlefield at twilight.

The next bedroom looked out upon a busy city at false dawn.

The third was held at midnight with the full moon shining in. There was something about the moon that chilled him.

He had no more luck as he traveled from room to room—drawing rooms, game rooms, libraries, and bedrooms. But none of the rooms housed the captured fae.

He had not believed it would be that easy, but he had hoped that just perhaps...

The Woodcutter sighed and sat down in the never-ending hall of marble and gilt frames.

He wiped his hands upon his jerkin, leaving trails of sparkling white dust.

CHAPTER 40

He watched the Twelve Ladies step into the hallway, delicate dancing shoes upon their delicate feet. The Ladies' eyes were ringed with circles and their faces deeply lined from lack of sleep. Even so, they laughed, delighted to be at the party.

He followed them from the day-lit hallway into the ballroom kept in eternal night.

The Gentleman waved his fingers at the Woodcutter from the piano, making sure the Woodcutter knew his presence had been noted.

Over the laughter and the clinking glasses, Jack's voice drifted sleepily. "Mother, I am so tired. Can we go home now?"

The Woodcutter found them at once in the crowd and watched them like a lion in the tall grass.

Jack leaned wearily against the Queen, his skin ashen.

The Queen looked at Jack, her earlier delight at the boy now turned to disdain. "Don't you see that Mother is speaking with her friends right now? Don't be rude."

"But Mother—"

"I said don't be rude."

"But I'm so—"

She cut him off as the back of her hand struck him across the face. "SILENCE!"

And the Woodcutter was there. He ripped Jack away from the Queen, pushing her aside. The ballroom stopped.

The Woodcutter stood, a mighty oak, his hands protectively shielding Jack.

Jack's eyes cleared for a moment, and he looked at the Woodcutter, looked and remembered. And then the spell descended once more. Jack ran to the Queen, screaming, "Run, Mother, run!"

Hatred flashed across the Queen's face as Jack gibbered at her side. She was dangerous, violent.

But she was nothing compared to the Woodcutter.

The Queen spat, "You are lucky you are who you are…"

The Woodcutter calmly unstrapped the Platinum Ax, River God be damned.

Two footmen scurried to the Queen's side.

She shrugged them off angrily, but her veneer of perfection cracked just a moment, revealing fear as the Woodcutter raised the Ax with two hands.

And then she laughed, falsely spirited, but her eyes never left the Woodcutter as she spoke to the crowd. "It's all right. We were just playing a game."

The Queen snapped her fingers.

The room returned exactly to the way it was before she had hit Jack, the music at the same note, the dancers at the same place.

"Mother, I'm so tired. Can we go home now?" Jack's voice drifted sleepily.

The Queen glowered at the Woodcutter before crouching before Jack. "My little one, don't you see? You are home."

Jack looked around in amazement. "I thought—"

"Now, darling, it doesn't matter what you thought. I'm sure you are tired. Why don't you crawl into bed?"

Jack gave her a hug and ran across the dance floor to a heavily cushioned window seat. He crawled up against the glass.

She snapped her fingers again and allowed the boy to sleep.

The Woodcutter strapped the Platinum Ax back at his side.

The Queen walked over to him and whispered in his ear, her long red nails upon his chest. "Do that again and—I don't care who you are—I will rip your still-beating heart out with my own hand and eat it later that day upon wheat toast."

As she walked away, the Dancing Lady of Orange swayed and fell drunkenly upon his back. "She'll do it too, you know," she slurred.

CHAPTER 41

Hour after hour.

Day after day.

The party did not end.

The Woodcutter continued to search the House, trying to find the hostage fae. Each time, the rooms shifted; each time, the hallways twisted; and each time, he always found himself returned to the doors of the ballroom.

Jack's eyes had become sunken.

But try as he might, whenever the Woodcutter tried to approach the child, the illusion of a wolf still veiled his true identity.

The Woodcutter sat in the corner, a pounding headache ripping through his skull.

The way out looked more and more attractive, but he had still found no sign of the captured fae, and if he left, he would lose the child. He could not risk Jack; he would not risk Jack.

But the dust was wearing away at his soul.

The only people allowed to leave the Vanishing House were the Twelve Dancing Ladies, but only when their dancing shoes had worn through. Hours later, they would appear with no memory that they had ever been in the Vanishing House before.

He would catch flickers of conversation as they danced by.

"That suitor will never figure out where we are…" said the Dancing Lady of Yellow to her sister of Green.

"One more fool who thought he could catch us…" said the Dancing Lady of Indigo.

The Woodcutter watched them night after night, their eyes glazed and unaware. He watched and wondered, wondered about their importance to the Queen and the Gentleman.

He waited until one night when the youngest Dancing Lady, blonde curls cascading upon her bare shoulders, fell exhausted at his side. She leaned against him and gripped his arm as if the whole world were spinning.

"Truly…Is there any place that could be more fun?"

The Woodcutter lit his pipe.

"I have never danced like I have danced tonight. I think I wore through my shoes!"

"Better dancing than last night?" asked the Woodcutter.

She slapped his arm playfully. "Silly goose, what happened last night?"

"You were here dancing," he said.

"No, I wasn't. I came here tonight for the very first time as the special guest of the Queen."

The Woodcutter raised an eyebrow. "Really?"

The Lady's head nodded too emphatically. "Indeed. She loves me and my sisters. And she says that we are all really princesses."

"Really?"

"Indeed."

"Princesses?"

"Princesses."

"I thought you had to be born with blood that runs blue to be royalty," said the Woodcutter.

"That's how it used to be. But you see,"—she walked her fingers up his jerkin and tweaked his nose—"things change."

"Really?"

"Indeed."

"And how does this work?"

"Well,"—she wiped away a rivulet of drool that had escaped from the side of her mouth—"the Queen says false princesses have taken over the Kingdoms. Lots and lots of Kingdoms. Twelve in all. One got away and found a prince. But that's fine because another Kingdom magically appeared. Just like that."

She tried to snap her fingers.

"The universe is on the side of the Queen. It just wants her to be happy." She paused, her thought stream interrupted by an explosion of confetti at the far end of the dance floor.

The Woodcutter shifted in his seat.

"Right." She turned back to the Woodcutter, chattering, "The universe just wants the Queen to be happy, and what would make the Queen happy—and I know this because she told me—is to have me and my eleven sisters become princesses and rule the Twelve Kingdoms. She would be an empress, but not really. Just in case my sisters and me need help."

"And how is this going?" he asked.

"Oh, very well. She has captured just about everyone. Except there is this one princess that disappeared, and evidently, she is important. And this man who has an empire in the Wood, he holds things together, and they can't figure out how to get rid of him. The Queen is going to take over for him. Oh, and there are Thirteen Kingdoms now, but they are having trouble seating my sister on the new throne. They don't know why, but they are going to see if anyone else has blue blood in the Thirteenth Kingdom that we didn't know about. But otherwise it is splendid."

The Woodcutter tapped his pipe thoughtfully. "But how do they get your blood to run blue?"

The Dancing Lady leaned in excitedly. "Dust. Lots and lots of dust. We have to have dust with every meal. It really is lovely, and I don't know why everyone doesn't have dust all the time. Pretty soon, he"—she pointed at the Gentleman—"he's going to make dust fall from the sky and we'll have even more kingdoms. Or bigger kingdoms. Or no kingdoms or something. I don't know which. But they just have to find that girl and that man, and then it will be perfect."

The Woodcutter playfully brought his face close to hers. "Our host, I just keep forgetting…Do you know his name?"

She looked at the Gentleman through one eye as her body swayed. "No."

And her eyes rolled back into her head and she collapsed onto the floor.

CHAPTER 42

He did not know what price she would pay for the treachery of telling him, but he was grateful.

He leaned her unconscious form against the wall and rose to his feet.

They wanted the Kingdoms.

They wanted his Wood.

Many thought that he who controlled the Wood would control the faerie world.

He shook his head at their ignorance.

It was now time to leave, danger or not. He reached into his pack and removed the harp. The golden lady stretched like a waking kitten in the candlelight of the ball.

"Would you do me the honor?" he asked.

The harp bowed her head.

The Woodcutter brought his hands to her strings, and she began to sing a sweet song that felt like a warm blanket on a cold night.

The Gentleman's head snapped to attention, even as his eyes began to droop. The Woodcutter could feel him try to wrap a magic spell about him, but too late...too late...

The Queen yawned. "Destroy the harp!"

Even as she sank sleepily to the floor.

Even as the whole room sank to the floor.

They slept.

Everyone slept.

And for the first time in weeks, the night shifted to day.

The painted faces could not hide their fading colors.

The Woodcutter spoke as he continued to play. "Milady, I need a song that will make those with blue blood sleep, even when your song has faded."

Once more, she bowed her head.

This time, the song was dark and drowning.

Breathing slowed.

Faces faded from pink to gray.

The Woodcutter played on, played until the final note and the harp's voice died away.

The harp gave him a nod and then closed her eyes.

The Woodcutter gently placed the harp back in his pack. He picked his way through the crumpled forms on the dance floor to the sleeping Jack upon the sill.

He leaned over and gathered up the child and held him close to his heart.

Together they left the house.

CHAPTER 43

The Woodcutter reentered the forest.

The trees became thicker and moved their roots to hide the Woodcutter's steps.

The Woodcutter stopped when the wind no longer carried the taint of the Vanishing House and placed Jack gently upon the ground. Jack's breathing was slow and steady. His golden-brown curls lay thickly across his untroubled brow. The shadows had lifted, and his eyes seemed not as sunken.

The Woodcutter patted him upon the cheek to try and wake him, but Jack still slept.

A night.

And a day.

And the night had come once again, but still Jack had not stirred.

The darkness was kept at bay by the cracking fire the Woodcutter built to keep Jack warm. The Woodcutter smoked his pipe thoughtfully, staring at Jack and waiting for the answers to make themselves known.

He looked up at the sky as the smoke rose, twisting and turning and bringing with it a disturbing warning.

The Woodcutter stood, troubled by what he had seen. He walked to Jack's side and took the boy's hand in his own and pricked Jack's finger.

Blue.

The child bled blue.

Blue from the dust storm that had anointed Jack's mother as Queen of the Thirteenth Kingdom, crowned moments before her death.

Blue because, with her death, the magic transferred to Jack, making him the heir and ruler.

The Woodcutter held his handkerchief to Jack's finger, watching the blue seep into the fibers.

Inherited blue blood never faded.

The Woodcutter sat down upon the ground heavily. He had not thought that Jack would turn, but the child had held his mother and wept powerful tears over her corpse.

The magic had found its path.

And now he slept as a blue-blooded victim of the harp's spell.

The Queen and the Gentleman had not calculated on there being an heir. The Queen and the Gentleman would stop at nothing to recapture Jack once they made the discovery.

And Jack, with his unclaimed heart, was now prey for the Beast.

The Woodcutter reached with his senses, straining to hear the first heavy steps of the hellhound's paws. The fact they had survived this long was a miracle. He knew he could not protect the child and also stop the Queen and the Gentleman.

He watched the gentle rise and fall of Jack's chest.

He would have to leave the child.

The survival of the entire human race depended upon it.

But he could not lose another to the Beast, especially a child who came back for him when he could have climbed down a beanstalk to safety, a child whose mother died because the Woodcutter had given three magic beans to a peddler, a child who had trusted him…a child he had failed.

There was only one bit of magic that the Woodcutter could do to protect him. It was not enough, but it was all that he could do.

The Woodcutter turned to the trees and whispered. They caught the whisper and murmured it back and forth to one another.

He rubbed together his hands, and they whispered, *Yes.*

He blew upon his fingertips, and sparkling earth magic followed the path of his whisper, landing upon the trees' branches, giving them the power to step outside the boundaries of nature.

Slowly they began to move.

Gracefully, playfully, they swayed to unheard music. Faster, they captured up the sleeping child to cradle him like a newborn babe in their intertwining branches. Soft moss sprouted and grew to build a blanket and a soft pillow for Jack's head. Vines spread between the branches of the trees, forming a woven wall that grew thicker and thicker until the child could no longer be seen.

The Woodcutter stepped back.

A rumbling shook the ground beneath his feet, a rumbling that erupted into a fortress of thorns. They sprang from the earth, followed by a surge of sharp, jagged rocks. With rocks and thorns, they formed an impenetrable wall.

And Jack was gone.

Claimed by the forest.

The Woodcutter stared at the protective prison, the hidden castle surrounded by a briar patch of deadly roses, and he felt a part of his heart leave itself with the boy.

He had once called Jack "son."

His wife had stared so many nights at the lonely road before their small cottage, hoping and praying that their child would arrive.

And the child never had.

The Woodcutter bowed his head and whispered to the leaves, "Let no one pass save this child's true love, who will part the thorns with her step and wake his spirit with true love's first kiss."

The leaves gently rustled in agreement, binding the pact.

The Woodcutter whispered, "Good-bye."

He knew he would never see Jack again.

CHAPTER 44

He walked far from the fortress that now guarded Jack, as far and as fast as he could, as if monsters nipped at his heels, until finally, swaying with hunger, he sat down.

He opened his pack, his heart heaving.

He opened his last journey cake, the last bit of food packed by his wife. He ate it slowly until he looked down and all that was left was one bite.

The last physical proof he carried of her touch.

He placed the dry bread in his mouth, letting it melt slowly upon his tongue.

And then it was gone.

His hands were empty.

Gone.

He looked up at the trees, the tall, slender trees that never touched except for their branches.

He heaved a sigh that seemed to echo to the very depths of his being.

And there, alone in the forest with no human soul to hear, he wept.

CHAPTER 45

The trees there knew him by name. They whispered in greeting, in hushed excitement.

"What did you learn?" they begged.

The Woodcutter exhaled, and on the wings of that breath, his story unfolded.

The leaves of the aspen shivered silver and sage. The pine's cones fell in fear.

The Queen, the Gentleman, they shook.

But the Woodcutter would not stop, could not stop to whisper hope to his friends, for he knew each footstep brought him closer to his doom.

He had spoken to the Crone, and she had told him the future of anyone who dared to face the Beast.

His feet could not stop until they reached the end of the path.

So he walked on, a day and a night, and a night and a week, until he reached the inn, the inn he had rested in that first night so long ago.

He walked to the tavern and laid his wooden coin upon the counter.

The barkeeper did not look up from his wash. "Your money is no good here, Woodcutter."

The Woodcutter walked up the stairs and into the whore's bedroom.

She lay sprawled upon the purple coverlet.

She lifted a drooping lid. "I don't work tonight. Find yourself another room."

But he would not be turned away.

He sat down upon the chair. "Who are you?"

The woman turned and pressed her face into a pillow. "Didn't you hear what I said? Leave me alone."

"Who was your daughter's father?"

She glared at him and reached her hand toward her dust box. "I have no daughter."

The Woodcutter remained silent.

"Are you still here?" she asked.

Still he remained.

She lifted her head and growled at him, "Why won't you go away?"

"Who is your daughter's father?"

"Some noble. Are we finished?" she replied.

The Woodcutter felt his blood run cold within his veins.

"And do you have any other children by this man?" he asked.

Her eyes were glazed, and her head lolled back upon a tasseled pillow. She ran her fingers through her mess of blonde curls. "It was so long ago…"

"Another child?"

A trickle of red bled from her nose. She lifted the back of her hand carelessly to stop the flow.

It spilled upon her fingers and dripped down upon her forearm.

The Woodcutter pulled a handkerchief from his pocket and pressed it firmly to the blood. She barely lifted her eyes to him, but smiled in gratitude.

"It was so long ago," she whispered. "I never told anyone."

"What didn't you tell?" he murmured back.

"About my other daughter."

CHAPTER 46

He stepped out of the brothel and lit his pipe, thinking back to the conversation.

A sister.

    A sister to the half-blood.

    A sister with the same blood.

    A sister who would be killed as soon as she was discovered, because she, like her unknowing sister, was the next rightful heir of the Ninth Kingdom.

    "And where is this sister now?" he had asked the woman.

    The mother's eyes closed as oblivion enveloped her. "East of the sun and west of the moon."

The embers of the Woodcutter's pipe shone orange in the dusk.

CHAPTER 47

The tree was silent and dark, like a hole in the forest. It did not murmur to its friends. It did not answer the Woodcutter when he called out to it.

It stood like a warning.

A small, round door and a small, round window fit themselves into the gnarled trunk. The Woodcutter placed his hand upon his father's ax. The fae were not always good. He knocked upon the tree.

A short little man with wiry red hair opened the door. He wore a rust-colored tunic, a fine gold necklace, and a lady's ring. The dwarf's eyes were dark and beady and regarded the Woodcutter with suspicion.

"What do you want?" he wheezed in a high-pitched voice.

"I seek shelter for the night," said the Woodcutter.

The dwarf held the door. "And what is it you would pay me with for such a service?"

The Woodcutter tried not to stare at the jewelry shining gold against the dirt caked into the pores and crevices of the dwarf's neck and knuckles.

"I have a fine pipe, which I would gladly share," offered the Woodcutter.

The dwarf wrinkled his nose as he considered the bargain and then stepped aside.

The hovel was far larger than the tree it was within, but the walls were still wood and the floor was still dirt. Roots had grown up out of the earth and twisted upon themselves to form chairs and tables. A cold fire burned without wood or coal in the hearth.

The dwarf settled himself in his chair and glared at the Woodcutter. "So what is this you say about a pipe? I suppose you have matches and fire?"

The Woodcutter opened up his pack. As he bent over, he commented upon the dwarf's necklace and ring.

"Those are quite fine," said the Woodcutter.

The dwarf stroked his jewelry possessively. "Indeed, they were the gifts from a princess for services rendered."

The Woodcutter looked at the dwarf sharply.

Far too many were mingling in the affairs of the Twelve Kingdoms' royalty.

"And what services did you provide?" he asked casually.

The dwarf laid a finger aside his nose. "Ah, 'tis a secret, human."

The Woodcutter pulled out his pipe and his tinderbox. The dwarf licked his lips, eyes never leaving the Woodcutter's hands.

The Woodcutter stopped, aware of the dwarf's intent interest. "I suppose I should just light my pipe by your fire?" he said.

The dwarf shook his head. "No, no, you must light it with your fire. Your warm, consuming fire…"

The Woodcutter took a match from his box and lit it. The dwarf held out his hands and closed his eyes, enraptured with the heat. The Woodcutter let it burn itself out.

The dwarf's eyes flew open. "Where did it go? You must bring it back! You must bring it back now!"

"Of course," said the Woodcutter.

He lit another match and this time lit the pipe and handed it over to the dwarf. The dwarf puffed on the pipe like a suckling babe. When he finally got his fill, he leaned back and exhaled. The smoke filled the entire house.

The Woodcutter stroked his beard. "I can see, friend, you are a fine connoisseur of flame."

The dwarf licked his lips again, staring at the embers inside of the pipe.

"Perhaps you would like a larger fire?" said the Woodcutter.

The dwarf looked at him in awe. "You would give me fire?"

The hair on the Woodcutter's neck stood up in warning.

"I will share my fire, but in the morning, you must give it back," said the Woodcutter.

The dwarf agreed, "Indeed! Indeed, I have been so cold, so cold since I was forced to live above the ground. Name your price!"

The Woodcutter pretended to think. "Let us not talk of business now. It will take me a while to build the fire. Let us go outside, and while I work, we can talk of what might be an appropriate settlement."

The dwarf nodded greedily. "Indeed! Let us go outside and discuss! You are a wise man indeed!" He patted the Woodcutter's arm in excitement. "Out we go!"

While the Woodcutter dug the fire pit into the earth, he sent the dwarf out to gather dry, dead branches from the ground. Soon a bonfire taller than a man roared, rising up into the night sky.

The dwarf danced with glee, warming his hands and then his backside and then his hands again. "I thought I would never be warm again!" he exclaimed.

The Woodcutter left the clearing, giving the dwarf time alone with the fire. The dwarf began dancing, faster and faster until his feet blurred and his face glowed red.

The dwarf sang out in joy, drunk from the flames as they rose and leapt: "*Little coals, little embers, tonight you dance for me! Fire taken away for greed, now you feed upon the tree!*"

The Woodcutter rested his hand upon a tall pine. The tree leaned against him and whispered for him to wait.

So he waited for an hour and then an hour more, watching as the dwarf fed the flames, as he continued his songs of nonsense and songs of love, as the world ceased to exist beyond the light of the blaze.

But then the tree leaned forward, and so the Woodcutter leaned in too. The dwarf began a new song as he swayed in the heat: "*Today do I bake, tomorrow I brew, the day after that the Princess comes in, and oh! I am glad that nobody knew that the name I am called is Rumpelstiltskin!*"

The tree shifted. The time for waiting was done.

The Woodcutter returned to the clearing and dropped a load of dead branches into the bonfire. Rumpelstiltskin let out a whoop and leapt ten feet over the top of the flame.

The Woodcutter settled his back against the tree to smoke his pipe, watching the dwarf as he danced. The Woodcutter tapped out the ashes from his pipe and filled it again. Offhandedly he asked, "What was the favor you granted the Princess?"

Rumpelstiltskin looked back at the Woodcutter. "I shan't tell."

The Woodcutter's eyes bored into the dwarf. "It is the price I ask for the fire that you have danced around."

Rumpelstiltskin looked at the fire with such longing and then at the Woodcutter and then at the fire again. He waved his hands above his head in irritation. "Oh, she wanted to spin gold out of straw, so for two nights I did as she wished."

"And what happened on the third night?"

Rumpelstiltskin crept closer to the fire to bask. "I was told to bring her home with me."

"Who told you that?"

"A Queen dressed in red. She said to bring the girl to the Wood and to leave her for the monster to devour before bed."

"And did you?" asked the Woodcutter.

Rumpelstiltskin began dancing again. "Oh, I brought her here, but I'm smarter than that. Such a girl is worth a ransom, and I will find what the Queen values her at. So I brought her here, and here she stays, spinning gold from straw for the rest of her days."

The Woodcutter winked at him. "My, you are a sly one indeed. And very cunning too."

"Indeed, I'm a sly one. I'm a cunning, sly one."

"And where is she now?"

Rumpelstiltskin shook his head and leapt across the top of the bonfire again. "That information is worth much more than the fire that you shared. Give me what the Queen would pay, and I will tell where the girl disappeared."

"And what is the ransom?"

"I like babies. I like firstborn babies and fire," said Rumpelstiltskin as he cut a jig.

"I have neither to give you."

"Then you shall not have the Princess," said Rumpelstiltskin.

The Woodcutter looked at the trees, knowing why fire had been taken away from this dwarf. His greed grew with each crackling limb.

"What if I promised you her firstborn?" the Woodcutter said.

Rumpelstiltskin stopped. He licked his lips greedily. But then wagged his finger at the Woodcutter. "You cannot promise the child of another."

The Woodcutter leaned forward. "Well, you know that, and I know that, but the Princess is sure not to know. I shall tell her I was forced to strike a bargain. When she gives birth and you go to collect the child, I am sure you can trick her into it. You are so cunning and sly."

Rumpelstiltskin clapped his hands. "You're right. You are right indeed! I am a cunning fellow. Trick the girl and get a free baby in the bargain! You are right and have done me a favor."

He slapped his thighs and danced. He pointed off to a large boulder and sang to the blaze, "*We shall go that direction and walk until we reach a cave. She is inside, you'll see! And then, my dear fire, there will be babies for me!*"

The Woodcutter gathered up his things. Hypnotized once more by the inferno, Rumpelstiltskin swayed in the light and did not pay him any attention.

But just as the Woodcutter was about to step out of the clearing, he turned his head over his shoulder. "I almost forgot," he said. "Your name is Rumpelstiltskin."

Rumpelstiltskin stopped, and his face drained of all color. He turned to the Woodcutter and began screaming and pounding his feet. He pounded so hard that a crack of thunder boomed across the sky. And as the thunder boomed, he split in two and was swallowed up by the earth, never to be heard from again.

For true names in the mouth of an enemy have power.

The Woodcutter walked back over to the fire and shoveled dirt over the logs. Something gold caught his attention. He bent down and found the necklace and the ring in the scorched circle where Rumpelstiltskin had disappeared. He placed them in his pocket and then crawled up into a tree, falling asleep in the safety of his brethren's branches.

CHAPTER 48

The Woodcutter found the cave, just as Rumpelstiltskin had said. The entrance hid behind a large boulder covered in ivy and dead leaves. He felt along the rock, looking for a way in, but it kept its mystery.

A sound lifted his head to the sky, the sound of feathers and wings, and then of nails upon rock.

"Hello?" he called out as he backed away.

Above him, a four-legged creature dropped down upon the boulder. She had the head of a woman and the body of a lion and the wings of a mighty eagle and regarded him dangerously.

A sphinx.

Her golden eyes never left the Woodcutter as she paced the ledge above.

The Woodcutter rubbed his forehead wearily.

"You may ask a question and I will answer. And then I will ask a question, and if you do not answer correctly, I shall strangle you," she purred in her metallic voice.

The Woodcutter folded his arms. He had to construct the question just right.

"Very well," he said. "How shall I save the girl hidden here by Rumpelstiltskin?"

"You shall answer my question correctly, I shall die, and the rock shall open. Inside the cave, the girl spins gold from hay, and if you escape before the cave collapses, you shall save her," she replied.

She blinked at the Woodcutter.

"And now, my turn." She picked her teeth with a long, curved claw. "Which creature in the morning goes on four feet, at noon on two, and in the evening upon three?" she asked.

"Man," he replied.

She looked at him in shock, in rage, and then she cried a scream that rattled the rocks and caused the ivy to fall away. The sphinx's scream caused the boulders before him to split. She placed her feet inside her mouth to stop the screaming and began swallowing. She swallowed her feet and then her legs and then her torso and soon had eaten herself until nothing was left.

The Woodcutter brushed the dust from his beard and reflected on how sphinxes would live much longer if they asked a different riddle.

Inside was a brightly lit room that housed a girl with honey-colored skin and light-brown hair. She was chained to a monstrous spinning wheel. Her fingers bled blue as they worked, feeding the straw to the machine. Out the other side came a mountain of coins.

"Maid Maleen?" he asked.

She stopped, her eyes blank and glassy from exhaustion. She blinked and fell off her stool.

The Woodcutter ran to her side. He pulled a water skin from his pack and held it to her lips. She coughed and sputtered, but woke enough to drink a few mouthfuls.

He was contemplating how much time to give her to regain consciousness when a rumbling began shaking the ground.

The sphinx's cry had split more rocks than just the one hiding the girl.

The Woodcutter grabbed the key from off the wall and unlocked the chain that bound Maid Maleen. He scooped her up in his arms and raced out to safety.

CHAPTER 49

The entrance collapsed behind him as the Woodcutter ran out of the cave. He stood for a moment, looking at the rubble.

He placed Maid Maleen down in a bed of clover far from the cavern's entrance and shook her gently.

Her eyes fluttered open and fixed upon the Woodcutter. "Where am I?" she whispered.

"You are in the Wood," he said as he glanced around. The words of Rumpelstiltskin rang in his mind. The Queen had kidnapped the girl as food for the Beast. He did not know how long it would take for the hellhound to track them.

"We must leave the trees as soon as possible. We are in danger," he said.

She pushed herself up and swayed on her feet.

The Woodcutter caught her around the waist. She was exhausted and famished.

"Come along," he said. "Lean upon me for strength."

She was too tired to even question.

By the time they reached the edge of the trees, the Woodcutter was carrying the girl upon his back, but the Woods were large and the Beast had not appeared.

The Woodcutter stopped by the edge of the road and set the girl down in the tall grass. Maid Maleen had slipped in and out of consciousness the entire journey. He forced her to swallow more water and to eat a few bites of food he had gathered from his time in town, and then he allowed her to sleep.

He woke to the sound of marching feet and tinny trumpets blaring. The Woodcutter sat up and shielded his eyes with the back of his hand. The morning sun smiled upon a procession of gaily clad players.

A large man in green tights held up his hand and halted the group in front of the Woodcutter and the girl.

"Can we be of assistance?" the Lead Player asked.

The Woodcutter rose to his feet as the girl began to wake. "Just resting for the night," said the Woodcutter. "Where are you headed?"

A scrawny acrobat in turquoise flip-flopped to the side of the Lead Player. "He asks where we're headed...Why, to the capital city, of course! To play for the King on this most happy occasion!"

"And what happy occasion would that be?" asked the Woodcutter.

The Turquoise Acrobat shook his head. "You would think you had been lost in the Wood, the way you talk. To the marriage ceremony of his only daughter!"

The Woodcutter searched his memory. "The King of the Eleventh Kingdom has no daughter."

"She has been found!"

The Eleventh Kingdom had its daughter replaced by a changeling some sixteen years before. The real child had never been recovered.

Maid Maleen woke, and the Woodcutter took her hands and helped her to stand.

Her fingers were so small against his palm.

Her fingers were still stained blue from her work at the spinning wheel.

"If we might, we would travel this road with you. That is where we are going too," said the Woodcutter.

They walked with the merry troupe, and the girl seemed to have gained some strength. Maid Maleen was not the frail sort. Her arms were muscled from work, and her body was sturdy from use.

She looked over at the Woodcutter and smiled. "I have not had an opportunity to thank you for saving me."

"I made a promise to someone to find you," he replied.

"Who?" she asked.

"There is a duke in the Land of the Ordinary who said he fell in love with a girl who could spin straw into gold."

Her face flushed. "I do not ever wish to see him again."

"Why do you say that?" asked the Woodcutter.

She picked a wildflower that was growing upon the side of the road and picked off its petals one by one. "He locked me in a tower and said if I did not spin straw into gold, he would kill me."

The Woodcutter stopped. "He did not seem someone who would threaten death for gold."

"His advisor came and locked the door himself. He said he acted on behalf of the Duke."

"I promise, if what you say is true, justice will be meted," he said gravely.

The Woodcutter felt his coat pocket become heavy. He reached his hand inside and withdrew the ring and the necklace. "I believe these belong to you," he said.

The girl took the ring but shrank back from the necklace. "I will not take that. It was a gift from that duke."

The necklace glistened in the sun. The Woodcutter placed it in her palm and curled her fingers around the chain. "It may still be of some use."

She stood for a moment, her hand clasped in the Woodcutter's, but she did not turn and fling the necklace deep into the forest. Instead, she placed it around her neck and walked on.

CHAPTER 50

The stage was set and a crowd had gathered. An excited murmur rippled through the shifting bodies.

"Would you look at her!" whistled the Turquoise Acrobat as he peered through the curtains at the audience.

He stepped back and allowed Maid Maleen to take his place.

"That is the King's daughter?" she asked.

A bony girl with a bulbous nose sat on a chair before the stage. The princess was dressed in purple. Her face was narrow and sharp. Her eyes stuck out of her skull awkwardly, and her skin was leathery and webbed with broken, purple veins.

"Just as ugly as everyone has said. Looks like a nasty dust habit too. You can only stay on the dust for so long before it wrecks your skin. It's why I never touch the stuff." The Acrobat stretched, one leg touching the back of his head. "Maybe the King should have kept the changeling."

"You are awful," Maid Maleen laughed as she opened the curtain for another look.

The Woodcutter walked up behind her and placed his hand upon her shoulder. She turned, and he gave her a cupful of water. Maid Maleen gratefully smiled as she took a sip.

The crowd burst into applause as the Lead Player finished his introductions.

Maid Maleen handed the cup back and took a deep breath before stepping out onto the stage.

The Turquoise Player nodded his head as Maid Maleen's song drifted through the marketplace. "Lovely," he commented.

When she finished, the audience erupted into rowdy applause. Her face was flushed as she came back behind the curtain.

The Woodcutter smiled. Maid Maleen had insisted upon repaying the troupe for their kindness, and this was the arrangement she and the Lead Player had settled upon. It seemed an equitable resolution for all parties.

The show continued on, but as the players made their final bows, the audience became hushed. The Woodcutter walked to the curtain.

A female voice filled the silence. Her words were slurred as she loudly proclaimed, "As Crown Princess, whose royal wedding takes place in...someday soon..."

The Woodcutter felt a chill run through his bones. Her voice sounded familiar. He opened a tear in the curtain with two fingers and peered through.

The princess was turned toward the crowd. She swayed as she continued. "I declare this a fine troupe, and they shall entertain us at my wedding. Especially that singing girl. I say so. And so it shall be."

She flung her body at the aisle and weaved her way toward the castle, retinue falling in line behind her.

Maid Maleen turned to the Woodcutter. "I have been requested at the royal wedding?"

"Not bad for your first day of work," said the Turquoise Acrobat.

The Woodcutter wondered how the Purple Dancing Lady had become the Crown Princess and how the Queen and the Gentleman had slipped in the imposter.

CHAPTER 51

The castle was buzzing in preparations for the wedding. Maid Maleen's eyes looked as if they could not absorb enough of what was going on.

She carried in the last of the players' costumes when a servant curtsied before her and said, "The Princess sends for you."

Maid Maleen looked at the Lead Player. He shooed her away with his hand.

The Woodcutter tried to reach for her, to whisper a warning, but the servant had hurried her off down the hall.

He watched her as she went.

The Woodcutter sat upon a chair in a hallway waiting, his pipe lit as he stared at the paintings on the ceiling. He heard Maid Maleen coming, heard the swift swish of her skirts and her pounding feet.

She knelt down beside him and pressed her head into his knee. "Oh, Woodcutter, what shall I do?"

He looked down upon her face, streaked with tears.

"Now, child," he said as he smoothed her hair and lifted her chin, "what causes you such sadness?"

"The Princess," she replied.

"Why?"

He knew why. The rings had spoken, but he waited patiently as she explained.

"She says the Duke will not marry her if he sees her, and so she said I must take her place. She wants me to dress in her clothes and go through the ceremony for her, and when I return, we shall switch places again."

Her eyes filled once more with tears.

"And what did you say?" the Woodcutter asked.

"What could I say? She said she would kill me if I did not. She said that she would kill me if I told anyone. I had to say yes."

The Woodcutter placed his pipe back into his mouth and stared at the rings. They never lied.

"Well, you have made a promise. And that which you promise, you must perform."

And he would say no more.

CHAPTER 52

The Woodcutter stood beside the King in the courtyard. Flowers and ribbons adorned every arch. A long red carpet marked the wedding party's path to the church.

The King pounded the Woodcutter's back. "We are honored, so honored, and pleased to have you bear witness to the wedding of our daughter."

The Woodcutter bowed his head. "The honor is mine. This is a blessed day. Your daughter is lovely indeed, and it is well time that she should come home to her true family."

The King sighed and placed his hand upon his heart. "If only her mother were here to see this day. It killed her, the changeling did."

"I imagine it was quite a shock," said the Woodcutter.

"No," said the King, momentarily flustered. "I mean, the changeling killed her. Happened while she slept. It was quite tragic."

The Woodcutter looked at him sharply. "Why did you not send for me?"

The King shook his head. "After my wife died and the unpleasantness of disposing of the creature...It was just too much..." His brow became furrowed. "Actually I have no idea why we never sent for you. It seems like something we should have thought to have done."

The Woodcutter caught the smell of something, just the smallest breath of dark magic. There was just the slightest glaze to the King's eyes. To the casual observer, it might have appeared that the King was merely exhausted.

But the Woodcutter was not a casual observer.

"How were you reunited with your daughter?" asked the Woodcutter warily.

The King's round face lit up. "She appeared on our doorstep, bedraggled and soaked to the bone. She passed the pea test and had the mark upon her arm. Besides, a father knows his own daughter." The King began patting his doublet. "Speaking of... Where did I put my glasses?"

They hung from a chain around the King's neck.

Two trumpets blared, interrupting the conversation.

The Duke from the Land of the Ordinary entered the room. His eyes met the Woodcutter's, and his face flushed with excitement and hope.

The King let out a happy sigh and then noted to the Woodcutter with a touch of pride, "That duke sent word far and wide, looking for his true love. Did you know my daughter could spin straw into gold?"

The Woodcutter watched Maid Maleen as she stepped across the courtyard. "Yes, yes, I did."

She was dressed in the finery of the bride, face covered in a white veil. Jewels upon her dress glistened in the light, but the Woodcutter noted that, on her finger, she wore her old ring, and upon her neck, she wore her golden necklace.

There was a moment when time stood still.

The Duke's eyes fell upon Maid Maleen, and her eyes fell upon his.

The Woodcutter felt the wild magic build as the two walked toward each other. He felt it build as one hand reached and the other hand reached back. He felt the wild magic sigh at the contact.

But just as the wild magic should have been quieted and tamed, he felt the tension build once more as a sad tear slid down Maid Maleen's cheek. He felt her withdraw her feelings.

She believed she and the Duke could never be joined.

The Woodcutter hid his smile in his beard.

He followed the wedding party closely to the chapel. They marched throughout the city so to give the populace a view of the festivities.

Maid Maleen stared straight ahead, not daring to look at the Duke. Her face was sad and her footsteps slow.

The Woodcutter closed the distance between them as her lips began to move.

Instead of words, she began singing to the plants along the path. Her voice was heavy and sounded like her heart might break. "*Oh, nettle-plant, little nettle-plant, what dost thou here alone. I have known the time, when I ate thee unboiled, when I ate thee unroasted*," she sang.

The Duke turned to her. "What is it that you sing?"

She immediately stopped and cast her eyes down to the ground. "Nothing, just thinking of a girl called Maid Maleen."

"But you are she," said the Duke, searching her face.

"No, you are mistaken. You marry the Crown Princess," she replied.

A few minutes later, Maid Maleen began singing once again, a wandering tune of no matter. As they passed over the footbridge to the church, she sang, "*Footbridge, do not break, I am not the true bride.*"

Once again, the Duke stopped her. "What is it that you sing?"

Maid Maleen stuttered, her face drained of color, "I speak nothing. I sing a song of nonsense. I was only thinking of one I once knew named Maid Maleen."

He touched her hand gently, and they continued on.

They stepped up the stone stairs to the church. Cheers erupted from the crowd. Inside, the waiting guests came to their feet.

But Maid Maleen paused. She ran her fingers across the oaken door of the church and sang quietly, "*Church door, break not, I am not the true bride.*"

The Duke turned, beckoning her to join him inside the church. She did not move, but kept her hand upon the door.

The King squinted at Maid Maleen and looked at the Woodcutter. "I say, the blushing bride is a bit reluctant." He toddled over to her. "Come now, sweet daughter. All brides are a bit frightened on their wedding day. In you go. You look more radiant than I have ever seen. Don't be shy. The Duke awaits."

The Woodcutter stepped behind Maid Maleen and placed his hand upon her shoulder. "That which you promised, you must perform." Then he whispered, "Do not fret. True love shall conquer all."

She smiled sadly, looking at the Duke. "You know not whom you wed."

The Duke touched the delicate golden chain that hung around her neck. "The woman who wears this necklace is indeed my true bride."

Maid Maleen offered no more resistance. She stepped slowly into the church.

The Woodcutter took his place in the procession down the aisle.

Heads bowed in respect as he walked by, his father's ax hanging from his belt for all to see.

But he felt the same dark taint, a sense carried on the wind that all was not as it seemed.

Then he saw in the gallery of honored guests the shapes of the Queen and the Gentleman. Surrounding them were eleven Dancing Ladies, dressed in the colors of the rainbow.

The Queen's white skin flushed red as she stared at Maid Maleen.

And the Woodcutter smiled twice in one day.

The wedding went quickly, and the party returned to the castle. The Duke left for his chambers to dress for dinner, his eyes never leaving his bride. Maid Maleen, still veiled as tradition dictated until the bride's wedding night, walked like a woman condemned toward the chambers of the Purple Dancing Lady.

CHAPTER 53

The Lead Player clapped the Woodcutter on the back. "I had no idea we shared the road with royalty. You should have told us, Woodcutter."

The Woodcutter smiled. "I am only a servant."

The Lead Player leaned forward and peered at the Woodcutter's waist and whistled. "So that is the ax of the Woodcutters." He stood back up. "Thought it would be bigger."

The Woodcutter laughed. "I have often thought so myself."

The Turquoise Acrobat interrupted their conversation. "Anyone seen Maid Maleen? She's supposed to sing tonight."

The Woodcutter placed a hand upon the Turquoise Acrobat's shoulder and pulled him in consipringly. "Just a request, from one traveling partner to the other. Tonight let Maid Maleen sing last for the wedding party."

The Turquoise Acrobat looked at the Lead Player for approval. The Lead Player shrugged his shoulders. "Seems we've been royally commanded. She goes last."

The Woodcutter shook their hands in thanks.

The Woodcutter was sitting in the hallway, looking at the smoke rings from his pipe, when the Duke bowed before him.

"Woodcutter, I beg your humble pardon. I did not know who it was that visited me that day so many weeks ago," the Duke said.

The Woodcutter grunted and patted the bench beside him, indicating that the Duke should sit down.

The Duke rubbed his stockinged legs nervously. "I do not know how, but you found her. You found my love. I know I did not believe you could, but you did. But of course you did, you being the Woodcutter..."

The Woodcutter took his pipe from his mouth and pointed it at the Duke. "Now, you may have married your true bride, but there is more going on here than meets the eye and reason enough to worry."

The Duke's face flashed confusion.

"But I have a plan," said the Woodcutter.

The Woodcutter walked into the banquet hall.

The Purple Dancing Lady's face was veiled.

The Woodcutter walked up to the head table. Representatives from all of the other Twelve Kingdoms stood, bowing as he passed. The Queen and the Gentleman inclined their heads, but their eyes spoke that only the crowd in the room kept the Woodcutter safe.

The Woodcutter sat himself at the King's right hand.

The King leaned over to the Woodcutter and whispered, "Is my daughter not just the loveliest you've seen? Takes after her mother's side of the family, she does."

The Duke's face was taut as the Purple Dancing Lady leaned against his arm. "And didn't we just have the most wonderful wedding? I can barely believe how happy I am. I will never forget taking those vows with you. Those vows were wonderful. And the church. It was such a lovely church with all of those people there. What lovely people."

The Duke turned to the Purple Dancing Lady. "And I too feel a deep sense of contentment, being joined at last with my true bride."

She tried to rub her nose against his, but he pulled back.

"Just one moment, my dear," he said. He placed his hands to his lips and winked. "You were so charming as we walked to the church, singing those songs so sweetly. What was the one about the nettles?"

She looked down at the Queen and the Gentleman, but they were too far away to offer any help. She turned back to the Duke. "A song about the nettles? Oh my. My mind has forgotten in all of the excitement of the day. Let me just get a quick drink to wet these parched lips, and then I'll answer."

The players came into the Grand Hall, and the Turquoise Acrobat stepped onto the stage.

The Purple Dancing Lady clapped her hands. "Oh, look! The entertainment has begun! I chose them myself as a wedding gift to you, my love."

The Duke took her hands in his. "Darling, what was the song?"

She waved him away, eyes fixated on the stage. "Oh, I don't remember. Something silly I made up. A song from my childhood."

"What you sang," said the Duke, "was 'Oh, nettle-plant, little nettle-plant, what dost thou here alone. I have known the time when I ate thee unboiled, when I ate thee unroasted.' Don't you remember?"

The Purple Dancing Lady shifted uncomfortably. "I remember it now."

Her eyes flashed angrily across the room, looking, the Woodcutter was sure, for Maid Maleen.

The Duke stroked the back of her hand with a finger. "I was meaning to ask you about that. You ate nettles unboiled and unroasted?"

She looked at him warily. "Indeed. It is one of my favorite foods."

The Duke smiled. "How fortunate! For your song inspired me so, and this night is so special, I took it upon myself to prepare you such a dish."

He motioned to a servant, who uncovered a tray full of nettles and set them before the Purple Dancing Lady.

"Oh, my. Nettles. What a...delicacy. Unfortunately, I am so full I couldn't possibly..." she said with discomfort.

The Duke's eyes flashed dangerously. "You will eat your nettles, or indeed you are not my true bride."

The King harrumphed. "Now what sort of behavior is this? Making my daughter eat nettles at her wedding feast?"

The Duke stilled him. "But she says they are her favorite, and I want my true bride to have her deepest desire."

The Purple Dancing Lady locked eyes with the Duke, but lost the battle of wills. So she took one and popped it under the veil and into her mouth.

Open mouthed, she chewed it, spitting out the spikes as she could. Blue-flecked spittle stained the veil.

The Duke bit into the rich, juicy steak on his plate. "And what was it that you said at the footbridge?"

She choked upon the hard flesh of the plant. "Footbridge? I don't seem to remember. A drink. I must have a drink."

The Turquoise Acrobat was finished, and the Lead Player was upon the stage announcing the next act.

The Duke lifted his glass to the players as the Purple Dancing Lady called for a servant. "Surely you remember. You said, 'Footbridge, do not break, I am not the true bride.' Now why did you sing that? You said you would tell me later."

The Purple Dancing Lady gulped down the wine. "Just singing to myself. Evidently I do that. I sing without thinking."

The Duke leaned forward. "And what about what you said at the church door?"

The Purple Dancing Lady spat the last of the nettles surreptitiously into her napkin. The Duke raised an eyebrow. She explained, apologetically, "After all this time in the castle, they now scratch my gentle throat."

"Do you remember what you sang?" asked the Duke.

"I take thee for my husband?" she offered halfheartedly.

He shook his head.

And Maid Maleen stepped onto the stage and her eyes locked upon the Duke. She opened her mouth, and like a nightingale, her voice rang out, "I sang, 'Church door, break not, I am not the true bride.'"

The Duke rose from his seat, fixed upon Maid Maleen. "And then I said, 'The woman who wears this necklace is indeed my true bride.'"

He turned to the Purple Dancing Lady and demanded, "Where is the necklace?"

She sputtered and sprang from her seat in outrage, but Maid Maleen reached into her bodice and lifted the golden chain. The crowd began to murmur.

Maid Maleen held the necklace high overhead. "Here it is, my husband."

The Duke stood and pointed, declaring to the hall, "She that stands before you on that stage is the woman I married. She that holds the necklace is indeed my true bride."

The Duke lifted back the Purple Dancing Lady's veil, revealing her disfigured face.

The whole room gasped in horror.

The King squinted at Maid Maleen and then looked back at the Woodcutter in bewilderment. "How did my daughter get all the way up there? She was just here having dinner with her husband. My goodness."

The Purple Dancing Lady screamed at the King, "I am your daughter! She drugged me and stole my things, and against all the laws that are good, she took my place at my own wedding! She should be burned at the stake!"

But Maid Maleen's hands still held the necklace that the Duke had given her such a long time ago.

The Duke leapt over the table and pushed past the servants in the middle of the room. He jumped up onto the stage and took her face in his hands. "You, my love, are my only true bride."

He lowered his mouth to hers and sealed their love in true love's first kiss.

And with the union of that first kiss, the Woodcutter felt the wild magic trapped in the Duchy of Plainness rush its way home to join with the magic in the Eleventh Kingdom. It swooped in like a crashing wave.

The Dancing Lady shrieked.

The Queen and the Gentleman stood, knocking back their chairs.

The Queen screamed, "To me!"

The room erupted into chaos. Servants threw off their robes to reveal weapons and leather armor. The King's men rushed forth to stop their attack upon the head table.

The Woodcutter loosed his father's ax from his belt.

"Your Highnesses!" the Woodcutter cried to the Duke and Maid Maleen as he gathered up the royal family.

The Duke grabbed Maid Maleen's hand, and they began running over the tables to reach the King. The Woodcutter met them halfway, swinging his father's ax and parting the attackers. The Duke pressed himself against the Woodcutter's back. "What is the plan?" he shouted.

The Woodcutter replied, "Take your bride and the King to safety."

Suddenly the Queen laughed a laugh that stopped the fighting and caused the hair on everyone's neck to stand up.

She spat at Maid Maleen, "You may be the true bride, but your line shall be all but barren! You shall have one daughter, and on her sixteenth birthday, she shall prick her finger on the spindle of a spinning wheel, and when she does, she shall fall down and die!"

The Queen waved her hands over the room and shouted three words.

A plume of smoke rose from the ground.

When the smoke cleared, the Queen, her Gentleman, and the fighting army had disappeared.

The silence of the room was filled with sobbing women and vacant chaos.

"Oh my," said the King, wringing his hands. "Oh my, oh my, oh my. This is not how wedding feasts are supposed to be."

The Woodcutter spoke to Maid Maleen and the Duke. "Do not fear the Queen's curse."

The Duke clasped Maid Maleen close to his heart. Stricken, he looked at the Woodcutter. "I have not had to deal with curses before."

The Woodcutter declared to the room in a booming voice, "The curse will die with the Queen's death, but if in the coming days the Queen does survive and this couple does give birth to a child and she is indeed a daughter, I shall send twelve faerie godmothers to ensure her safety. Do not fear the Queen."

The King looked over at the Woodcutter with such sadness in his eyes, looking at where the Purple Dancing Lady had disappeared. "So the girl was not my daughter?"

Maid Maleen parted from the Duke and went to the King, placing her hand upon his arm. "Courage. We shall find her yet."

The King patted her hand and then stopped, his fingers upon her ring. He looked down upon it and then searchingly into the face of Maid Maleen. "Where did you get this, child?" he asked.

"I do not know, for I have always had it," she replied.

The King's eyes filled and his arms opened wide. "My child... oh, my child...It is truly you!"

Maid Maleen look around, bewildered. "You are mistaken. My father is a baker who lives on the border of the Land of Ordinary."

"No, child, you are mine, stolen away from me and replaced by a changeling."

"I don't believe you," she said as she backed away.

"Look at your arm. You have a mark just as mine."

The King pulled back his sleeve and revealed a purple birthmark in the shape of a bird.

Maid Maleen looked at the Woodcutter fearfully. He nodded for her to do as the King asked.

She pushed back her sleeve, and there lay the sister birthmark.

The King turned to her, brushing away the tears. "I believe there is a wedding feast waiting for the Duke and my daughter, his true bride."

CHAPTER 54

The Woodcutter left the castle with a whistle on his lips.

Rapunzel and Prince Martin. The Duke and Maid Maleen. Jack, who slept soundly in the Wood. The Princess Snow White, who was in the care of the fae.

Four of the Twelve Kingdoms were safe from the Queen and the Gentleman. He would find the missing half-blood girl. He would visit two other Kingdoms to ensure their alliance.

And the Queen and the Gentleman would fail.

The sun shone across the empty meadow, nothing but bales of hay and farmland between him and the Wood.

The attack came without warning.

An arrow lodged itself in his shoulder, knocking him to the ground. He lifted his head and saw the Gentleman and the Queen emerge from behind one of the stacks. From another bale, four soldiers climbed out and, from another, yet another four. Slowly they stalked toward the Woodcutter, crossbows trained upon his heart.

The Queen laughed. "Gentle, my loves. We don't want him dead."

The Woodcutter struggled to his feet, hand feebly upon his father's ax. The world faded in and out as he tried to hide his sap and replace it with the illusion of mortal blood.

Through the fog, he thought he heard a cry come from the direction of the road. He thought he heard a voice shout, "Woodcutter!"

He saw the Queen and the Gentleman as they looked over their shoulders. There seemed to be a caravan of brightly clad players rushing fast across the field. There was a man dressed in green and a slender man dressed in turquoise. He watched as the two parties met, swords crashing and limbs flying. The man in green, a man he could now remember was the Lead Player, mouthed silent words to the Woodcutter. He seemed to wave his hands as if shooing the Woodcutter away.

The Woodcutter stared at the Lead Player's lips, trying to figure out why they waggled. The slender man in turquoise, the Turquoise Acrobat, flipped over the head of the man he was combating to reach the Woodcutter's side. He pushed the Woodcutter and shouted, "Run! Run, you old fool!"

So the Woodcutter ran.

He ran as fast as he could to the tree line of his Wood.

He heard the Gentleman cry out, "Get him! Kill him!"

His lungs burned and his muscles ached.

Still he ran.

If he could just make it to the tree line.

He felt an arrow pass overhead.

And then one grazed his arm.

His eyes clouded in pain.

He fell, his hands touching the earth.

But still he ran.

Ran like a hind being pursued by the hunt.

Arrow still in his shoulder, he doubled his speed.

CHAPTER 55

The Wood gathered him like a mother's arms.

The trees bent their boughs to block the way of those who might follow.

The Woodcutter did not slacken his pace. He ran deep into the heart of the forest, where few human feet ever trod.

Deep where the Wood would make sure any traveler was made aware that he was unwelcome.

It was in this solitude that the Woodcutter collapsed, collapsed beneath the pain of the arrow notched within his shoulder.

He collapsed and knew no more.

CHAPTER 56

The trees wrapped around him as the wound oozed. They held him, cradled him, shifted the paths of the Wood so any enemy would be led astray.

He could feel the humans test his border, test the protection of the trees.

The wound pulsed, and he knew he could not survive.

He reached to the arrow and yanked it out.

A rush of warm liquid spilled down his body as he trembled. He took off his jacket and tried to stop the flow of sap.

The world shifted as stars filled his eyes.

His lips whispered to any that might listen, "Help."

CHAPTER 57

He woke.
The moon hung full above him.
He struggled to his feet and fell.

CHAPTER 58

A strong wind blew from the north, pushing the clouds across the sky.

His eyes opened slowly and tried to focus as the world continued to shift, as the trees continued to protect him by moving their very roots.

He turned his head to the other side and rested his sight upon the unmoving path.

Iron-shod feet were upon it.

Iron shoes, shoes that could not be affected by the shifting of the forest. They were shoes that had been rubbed from the miles of traveling until there was barely a sole left.

Long brown skirts hung over the iron shoes, worn by a girl who seemed not a day over twenty, yet not a day under one hundred. The girl gasped as she saw his fouled form.

She dropped her walking staff and knelt down.

Her face was careworn, and her dark hair was streaked with gray.

She cradled his hand in hers. "Gentle sir, I did not expect to find anyone in these woods."

As she pulled away his jacket to examine the wound, the whole world went dark.

CHAPTER 59

He woke, covered by his own jacket and reclining upon his pack. His wound ached, but not like before.

The girl crouched by a fire, feeding the flames dry sticks. Her hands were stained with dirt.

She heard him stir and turned. Her chestnut eyes were lined with worry and concern. The Woodcutter stiffly pushed himself to a sitting position. She came to his side and helped him adjust until he was comfortable.

He moistened his cracked lips and his voice croaked, "You have saved my life, and I do not even know your name."

She smiled as she tucked his coat smartly around him. "It has been so long since I was called anything, I am afraid I no longer remember."

"It is the same with me," he said. "Those that know me call me Woodcutter."

She held out her hand. "You may call me Iron Shoes."

Her dirty hand, covered in his sap, stuck to his.

She rubbed her hand upon her skirt. "I am afraid that your blood must be magic, for it does not wash off my skin and it turns my hands brown instead of red. I hope you are not an evil faerie."

"No, Iron Shoes," he said as he regarded her. He could feel nothing menacing in her ways. "I am not evil, and I am not fae. I am one with the trees of this forest. My blood is the same sap that is theirs. That which flows through them flows through me."

She pulled back the dressing of his wound to see how it was healing. "I am sorry to have assumed. I had never seen anything like this before," she said as she pointed at his injury.

It had hardened, and around the cut, instead of a shiny pink scar, a knot of bark had grown and puckered.

"Is this normal for one who is one with the forest?"

He took her hand away and covered himself back up. "Indeed it is. You have helped more than you will ever know. I am in your debt."

She turned back to the fire. Balanced upon the coals was a metal pot, which spewed forth steam and lovely smells. She slid her feet out of her clog-like shoes as she stirred the pot. She looked over her shoulder at the Woodcutter's inquiring gaze. "My shoes heat when I stand too close to the fire."

"Why is it that you wear them?" he asked.

She paused before speaking, her gentle tone never changing, but her words seemed to come from far away. "I was married years ago to a great white bear and lived with him in a castle by the sea. He was, in fact, a man, but he was cursed by a witch he'd once offended. Each night, he would transform from a beast into my husband, but in the morning, he would return to beast again. After almost a year as his wife, I told my mother about his transformation and how it pained me to be parted from him during the hours of the light. She told me I must tie a golden thread to his ankle so that he might stay a man forever."

She heaved a heavy sigh.

"I did this, but when he woke that day, he cried out that if I had only been patient for three days more, the enchantment would have been broken and he would have been free forever. With these words, a great wind broke through the windows and stole my husband away."

She ladled the food onto two plates and brought one to the Woodcutter. "I went to an old seer to learn what had happened to my love, and she told me that the Sun would know where the wind took my husband. She predicted I would wear through three sets of iron shoes and an iron walking stick before I saw his face again. So I commissioned a blacksmith for such shoes and a stick and proceeded to walk to the Sun. But the Sun did not know. He thought that the Moon, who traveled so much closer to the earth, would have heard where to find my husband, so I walked to the Moon, but she did not know either."

Iron Shoes sat down beside the Woodcutter. "The Moon thought that the West Wind, who has traveled far across the ocean, would surely know of my husband, so I walked to meet the West Wind. But the West Wind had never heard of my husband or his new home. The West Wind kindly offered to carry me upon its back to meet the East Wind, since the East Wind could go places where it could not. But alas, the East Wind knew nothing of my husband. The East Wind thought perhaps the South Wind could help. The South Wind said it had heard from the North Wind of a strange journey involving a man who was a bear. In the coldest reaches of the earth, I met the North Wind, who said he had once been asked to carry a man to a land east of the sun and west of the moon. So the North Wind gathered me up and brought me to this forest, which is where you find me now, having worn through two pairs of iron shoes and with the last pair upon my feet."

There was a look on Iron Shoes's face, a look of such determination and love...

They had glared at each other in the great room of their cottage the night she learned who he was, the night she learned of his duties to the Kingdoms and that they could never have a child. She had shouted at him as he told her he would understand if she no longer wished to be his wife. She had clung to him, her face pressing his tear-soaked shirt against his heart, trying to get him to understand that she could never leave his side.

She picked them up and wiggled a finger through their soles. "I have worn through the third. So I must continue. I know my husband lives here somewhere. I must continue until I find the man I love."

His wife's sleeping face in the morning light. Even resting, she wore a smile...

He missed her so much it ached, and he saw the same ache in the lines that etched Iron Shoes's face.

"I shall help you through the Wood," the Woodcutter promised.

She shook her head. "Woodcutter, you should not have to involve yourself with my sorrow."

He stopped her. "I shall guide you until you reach the other side."

She rested her hand lightly upon his forearm. "Thank you."

CHAPTER 60

They had walked a week and a day and yet another week.

Her worn iron shoes allowed the branches and sticks to poke and cut her feet. Even her hardened calluses bled and cracked.

The Woodcutter helped her to bind them in the tattered rags of her shawl, but never a word of complaint left her lips, only hope and excitement that she might be drawing closer to her husband.

Three pairs of iron shoes worn through their iron soles.

On the first day of the third week, her walking staff broke, and they found themselves standing before a humble farm.

CHAPTER 61

The Woodcutter rapped upon the wooden door. The planks were smooth and worn from the years of protecting the home from the rain and wind.

Inside, the Woodcutter could hear the shuffle of tired feet, and the door opened to reveal a weary old woman with a toothless grin.

"Good evening, Grandmother. We seek shelter for the night," said the Woodcutter.

The old woman looked at them through one eye and then motioned them inside. Her joints and bones cracked as she walked. The one-room home was small and humble. Three animals lay by the hearth for warmth—a dog, a hen, and a brindled cow.

The Woodcutter caught the woman's elbow as she wobbled. She patted his hand kindly. "I am afraid that I am not able to offer much hospitality."

The Woodcutter set her by the fire and placed a blanket upon her lap. "Then rest, Grandmother. We do not wish to trouble you."

The cow lowed his opinion.

The old woman nodded in agreement and spoke to the Woodcutter. "Cook us our supper and you may stay until morning."

The Woodcutter reached down and patted the grizzled old dog. The dog licked the Woodcutter's hand and then settled his head back down between his paws.

Iron Shoes began moving around the kitchen, preparing a dinner from the items in the cupboards. The three animals stared at Iron Shoes pitifully.

The Woodcutter smiled at the animals. "Your empty bellies are not forgotten, my friends."

The Woodcutter went outside and found some hay and grain. He brought in the food and placed them before the cow and the chicken.

Iron Shoes put the food on the table and then ladled out a bowl of stew, setting it before the dog.

The dog lowered his head, and as his lips touched the food, a cracking sound echoed across the room.

The beams ripped themselves from the roof.

The walls groaned and grew, grew from humble plaster to marble columns and mirrors.

The Woodcutter leapt from the wooden chair, which had transformed beneath him to a delicate piece upholstered in white tapestry. He grabbed the confused Iron Shoes and pulled her toward the door.

"What is happening?" she cried.

"We must leave now!" shouted the Woodcutter. "The Queen. It must be the Vanishing House."

The room stopped rumbling, the transformation complete.

The floor was inlaid wood of complex scrolls and herring-bone. The ceilings were painted with visions of the Wood at sunrise. Gold cabinets and library shelves covered the walls. Soft, pale couches rested their slender carved legs upon lightly colored rugs.

The Woodcutter unstrapped his father's ax and stretched out his senses, prepared for danger.

A woman appeared in the doorway: a Lady with long golden hair that hung below her waist, a Lady dressed in light-blue gossamer who held out her hands to calm the Woodcutter and Iron Shoes.

The Lady in Blue stood, flanked by three servants. They bowed humbly before the Woodcutter and Iron Shoes.

One servant had liquid brown eyes. The other servant was round with mousy red hair that sat like feathers upon her head. The third servant had grizzled black hair and jowls that hung like a dog's.

The Woodcutter lowered his ax and smiled.

"Fear not, my gentle friends. I am the old woman you so kindly waited upon," said the Lady in Blue. Her voice was musical and danced like water upon the stones of a brook.

The Woodcutter walked to the Lady's side and embraced her warmly. "Queen of the Seventh Kingdom? Why did you hide yourself from me?" he asked.

The Lady in Blue held his hands in hers and gazed at him fondly. "Please sit and accept my true hospitality."

She perched upon one of the chairs and motioned for the Woodcutter and Iron Shoes to follow suit.

The servant with the liquid eyes walked over to a side table and poured drinks for the party. She offered the tray and asked in a low voice, "Iron Shoes?"

Iron Shoes took the glass and lifted it to her lips in bewilderment.

The Lady in Blue smiled at her servant and took a glass for herself as she explained, "A year ago, the Scarlet Queen from the Sixth Kingdom and her gentleman consort came to me with a vision of independence for the Twelve Kingdoms, to unite seven Kingdoms and break the treaty with the fae. But I knew that they truly wished to wield the power found in your Wood. My blue blood is not so removed that I am blind to the greed of man.

"I wove a spell to hide," she continued. "I knew my Kingdom would be safe as long as they could not find me, but I was worried the Queen would come in disguise and trick me with her words. My most trusted servants and I assumed the shapes you saw. Only when someone pure of heart came and cared for us, someone who waited not just upon an old woman, but also upon her strange companions with no hope of gain, only then would we return to our true selves."

The Woodcutter stroked his beard thoughtfully. "Why did you not contact me about this plot?" he asked.

"Because I could not." She stood and walked to the window. She opened the panes and pointed at the trees. "Their voices are quieting. The Queen and her Gentleman have captured too many of the pixies. The Queen and the Gentleman slowly bled the magic from my Kingdom until they were able to intercept all the messages I sent. I was cut off from all communication."

The Woodcutter reached out to the Wood, and the voices of the trees were muffled and weak. His mind began trying to put the pieces together.

The pixies. There were too many pixies captured.

The pixies were a conduit. They bathed the land in magic, baptized it in dust wherever they flew. The pixies watched and gossiped about the lives of humans endlessly with the trees. The Woodcutter was able to reach into the flow and know what was going on, but if there were no magic, if the stream slowed to a trickle, there would be no way of knowing if things were right or wrong.

The clouds…

The magic being taken from the Twelve Kingdoms…

The Woodcutter pointed to the sky. "That is why they took the magic. I thought it was the dust trade. Then, perhaps, to annex new kingdoms from the Land of the Ordinary. But it was to store the magic so that they could control the Kingdoms here."

"Annex new kingdoms?" the Lady in Blue asked in confusion. "There is not enough dust in the world…"

The Woodcutter shook his head. "I have seen it. There are solid clouds above us, fields of dust in the Cloud Kingdom. There was an accident with a beanstalk that caused the dust to snow upon a farm. It was enough to form a new Kingdom, the Thirteenth Kingdom."

The fear on Jack's mother's face as the Beast overtook her.

"The Thirteenth Kingdom," the Lady in Blue whispered.

The Woodcutter stood and began pacing the room. He brought his pipe out of his pack and lit it furiously, putting the pieces together. "But that was not their intention. I have been so foolish…"

His words came faster. "Whenever the clouds became too heavy and threatened to burst, the Queen and the Gentleman would let the dust fall upon the Land of the Ordinary, where the iron could dispel it. That, or the Queen and the Gentleman sold it to the dust trade."

The rings never lied.

And they told him what he spoke was true.

The Woodcutter leaned out of the window and stared at the sky.

He had to get the magic down. Without the pixies' magic he was blind, and blindness was what the Queen and the Gentleman of the Vanishing House wanted.

The Woodcutter understood.

"They tried to capture me," he said.

The Lady in Blue placed her hand upon his elbow in alarm. "If they had been successful, they would have had power over all the Twelve Kingdoms."

"Thirteen Kingdoms," he absently corrected, eyes still upon the starless heavens. "But they were not successful. They have shown their hand."

The Lady in Blue asked, "What do you mean?"

"When they tried to capture me, I learned that they had imprisoned six of the blue-blooded Princes who had not found true love."

The Lady in Blue tried to follow him. "Without true love, a Kingdom's allegiance to the treaty with the fae is thought tenuous."

"They brought in the Twelve Dancing Ladies to marry those Princes and to place upon the twelve thrones. They also lured a hellhound from the Wild Hunt," the Woodcutter said. "They began kidnapping the true Princesses and feeding them to the Beast."

The Lady in Blue looked at him squarely. "As long as they kept you blind, even if they could not capture you, as long as they could break seven of the Kingdoms from the treaty, they would have been strong enough to gain control over the remaining Kingdoms."

"In ruling the Thirteen Kingdoms and possessing all the magic they have stolen from the pixies, I believe they want to face King Oberon and Queen Titania," continued the Woodcutter.

"So that they can become the King and the Queen of the Fae," the Lady in Blue whispered fearfully. "They do not understand they are destroying themselves."

The Queen and the Gentleman.

Emperor and Empress of the Thirteen Kingdoms and seated in his Wood.

Their greed would undo them all.

The Queen and the Gentleman did not remember, or did not wish to believe the stories.

The Woodcutter looked at the Lady in Blue. "I have stopped them so far. They tried to take Princess Rapunzel, but she is joined now with her true love. Snow White is protected by King Oberon and Queen Titania. Jack rests in the Wood, protected by my trees. Maid Maleen has been married to the Duke and is acknowledged as the rightful heir. You have been returned to power."

The Lady in Blue looked at the Woodcutter's traveling companion, who had remained silent all this time. "Iron Shoes must succeed."

"Then six Kingdoms will be secure," the Woodcutter said. "I believe I know where to find the seventh."

The Woodcutter leaned forward toward the Lady in Blue. "I am looking for a human child with blue blood in her veins. She may not even know that she carries the ancestry of the fae."

Iron Shoes and a lost half-blood girl were the only hope against the Queen and the Gentleman.

The Lady in Blue nodded and walked to a desk. She pulled a large map from a cupboard and unrolled it upon the surface.

"You must cross this river and travel by foot along this path. Strange currents have come from around this area." She sighed. "As soon as you unite Iron Shoes with her husband, you must hurry. If I feel it, others must too."

The Lady in Blue turned to Iron Shoes and held out her hand. "Iron Shoes, your punishment for your impatience and the violation of the golden thread is almost through."

The Lady in Blue smiled at Iron Shoes's shock. "Yes, I know of what happened. I have been waiting for you for centuries, but I did not know that the role you must play is much larger than a simple search for the second half of your heart. You who have walked to the Sun and the Moon in search of true love, you who have ridden the back of the four Winds, you who have worn out three pairs of iron shoes and broken your walking stick to find the man you love—you have proven yourself worthy of your Prince."

Iron Shoes's breath caught in her throat. Her eyes filled with tears as she stared at the faerie queen in disbelief. "You know of my husband? You know where he lives?"

The Lady in Blue touched her elbow and said, "He is not far from here. He is enchanted and kept prisoner by an old woman named Baba Yaga."

The Woodcutter stopped puffing on his pipe.

"The Queen and the Gentleman have convinced Baba Yaga to marry your husband to a false princess, which will happen in three days' time," the Lady in Blue continued. "Tomorrow you must go to the castle of Baba Yaga and ask to serve as her seamstress. The only payment you will accept for your exceptional talent is to be able to spend the night with your love. It is only in the hours of darkness that your husband can see truth; it is only in the hours between midnight and dawn that he will recognize you."

"But I am not a seamstress," Iron Shoes said.

The Lady in Blue laughed, her voice sparkling in the air. "But you are."

The Lady in Blue stepped to a cabinet and opened up the golden doors. She pulled out a sewing basket. Inside were three golden needles and three spools of golden thread. "You are the only one that can wield these instruments, and with these instruments you shall save your true love. Gold thread tore you apart, and in three days' time, it will unite you once again."

The Lady in Blue turned to close the cabinet, but stopped herself. She reached up and brought out a bundle of brown material from another shelf. She handed it to the Woodcutter. "I was given this bag by a soldier who once captured death and held it for a time. I give it now to you. You have only to say, 'Get in my bag,' and whatever it is you wish to capture must jump inside."

The Woodcutter took the bag and placed it in his pack. "Thank you," he said.

"Yes, thank you," Iron Shoes continued fervently.

"I wish I could do more," the Lady in Blue replied.

The Lady in Blue closed up the cupboards as the servant with the grizzled hair bowed in the doorway. The Lady in Blue motioned to her guests. "Let us at least sit down to eat before you continue on your way."

When the meal was finished, the Lady in Blue pointed at the fish bones upon their plates. "Gather these up and place them in your napkins. They are my final gift to you."

CHAPTER 62

A strange castle sat before the Prince's palace, made of stone, round bottomed, with two chicken legs protruding from the tower walls. It looked as if the whole building had walked itself to the palace and then sat itself awkwardly before the gate.

Which it had.

Such was the nature of Baba Yaga's moveable castle.

The Woodcutter stood with Iron Shoes upon the threshold of the castle's kitchen.

Iron Shoes knocked upon the door, timid but resolute.

"Whaddya want?" a harsh voice bellowed.

The door opened, and before the Woodcutter and Iron Shoes stood Baba Yaga. Her face was warted and her iron-gray hair flew out in wiry tendrils. At her waist swung a sturdy ring of keys. Baba Yaga looked at the Woodcutter, and only the faintest glimmer in her eye gave away that she recognized him.

"Forgive me for disturbing you, Baba Yaga. I come seeking work," whispered Iron Shoes reverently.

"And what is it that you do?" she cackled as she looked Iron Shoes up and down.

"I am a seamstress."

The Woodcutter gently took her elbow in his hand. "Of remarkable skill."

"Remarkable skill, eh?" said Baba Yaga. She stroked her whiskery chin. "I have some mending that you might do. Very well, let's see your remarkable skills, seamstress."

She stepped aside to let Iron Shoes in, but held her arm out across the doorway and stopped the Woodcutter from following.

"And what is it that you do?" she asked. Baba Yaga was now fully the Crone, with no memory of the Maiden's kindness.

"I thread her golden needle," said the Woodcutter.

Baba Yaga wiggled a gnarled finger at the Woodcutter. "Seems like a job that can be handled by one. I don't pay wages to needle threaders."

"I work for the seamstress and require no additional wages beyond the wages she expects," replied the Woodcutter.

Baba Yaga turned to Iron Shoes. "And what are these wages you will be demanding?"

Iron Shoes touched her hand to her tattered shawl and spoke bravely. "A night with the Prince for every day's labor."

Baba Yaga looked at her slyly. "A night with the Prince. For a day's worth of my mending…Very well, we have a bargain."

Baba Yaga walked the Woodcutter and Iron Shoes to a tower room and threw open a door.

A mountain of laundry, from floor to ceiling, lay heaped upon the ground.

"You do all the darning, you do the darning so tight that not a thistle can slip through the seams, you do it all in a day, and I'll give you a night with the Prince. And if you don't, I shall cook you in my stew," said Baba Yaga.

She slammed the door closed with a wicked laugh, leaving the Woodcutter and Iron Shoes alone inside.

CHAPTER 63

Tears sprang to Iron Shoes's eyes as she stared at the pile of mending. "It is impossible."

The Woodcutter placed his hand upon her shoulder. "Courage."

He took the sewing basket from his pack and handed her the needle and thread. Her hands shook so that she could barely thread the gold through the gold, but the moment her fingers lay upon the first sock, it was as if it were sewn by magic. In and out, her fingers pushed the needle, faster than eyes could follow.

The Woodcutter stood, holding the spool as the thread disappeared.

And so as the sun set upon the first day, the thread ran out and the first spool lay in the Woodcutter's hand, empty. The first needle disappeared into the air.

The mending was done.

Iron Shoes looked at the Woodcutter, full of hope. "I shall see my true love."

Just then Baba Yaga stepped inside the door, wringing her hands with glee. "Well then, lass, seems there'll be a tasty dinner for me—"

And then she spotted the mending, and her face turned ashen.

"Girls!" she cried.

Two servants stepped forward, eyes downcast upon the floor.

"Go through this mending, and if there is a seam that should gap so much as to let a thistle through, you call me at once."

But no fault could be found in Iron Shoes's mending, even though it was almost midnight when the inspection was through.

Baba Yaga returned and leered at the girl. "I don't know how you did it, but a bargain is a bargain. Come, let us away to your Prince."

Iron Shoes looked back at the Woodcutter, eyes sparkling with joy.

Baba Yaga looked at the Woodcutter with disdain. "As for you, you can stay here until morning. You should have asked for boarding with your mistress's wage."

The Woodcutter sat in the dark as the last of the lantern light disappeared.

CHAPTER 64

He woke in the morning to sunlight upon his face.

Iron Shoes stepped into the room, tears streaming down her cheeks.

She rushed to the Woodcutter. "Oh, Woodcutter, I could not wake him. Try as I might, he slept as if dead. This was all in vain."

The Woodcutter stroked the young woman's hair and hushed her. "Today is a new day, and we still have two spools of thread. Despair not. Tonight you shall see your love."

She looked at him, wiping away her sadness with the back of her hand.

They stepped out of the tower room and into Baba Yaga's kitchen.

Foul stew sat boiling over the fire.

Baba Yaga looked at the twosome and gave a wicked grin. "Did you get all that you wanted in your night with the Prince? It seems I have some more mending if you are game."

Baba Yaga lifted a spoonful of the stew to her lips and gave Iron Shoes a knowing wink.

Iron Shoes straightened her back and spoke. "My services are available if there is work to be done."

"And what'll be your wage?" Baba Yaga spat.

"A night with the Prince," replied Iron Shoes.

"Very well," Baba Yaga said. "This stew is a bit runny for my taste, and I have some honored guests coming for the wedding." Baba Yaga threw down the spoon. "Come, let us get started."

She walked Iron Shoes and the Woodcutter to a second tower room that housed twice as many garments with twice as many rips.

"You shall mend my garments so that not a thistle can slip through the seams. You do this, and you shall have a night with your prince. If you do not, I shall cook you in my stew."

And with the bargain laid, Baba Yaga left.

The Woodcutter stayed only long enough to watch Iron Shoes thread her needle and to watch once more as her fingers flew.

He then stepped out of the room quietly, so as not to disturb her sewing.

The Woodcutter sat at the fire as Baba Yaga puttered around the kitchen.

She pretended to ignore him.

He lit his pipe.

She turned and gave him a glare. "That smoke of yours will ruin my dinner, Woodcutter."

He gave her a smile.

Baba Yaga spooned something vile into a bowl and threw it upon the table. "Taste and see."

The Woodcutter did not touch it.

Baba Yaga laughed. "Do you remember when you were too polite to turn down my cooking?"

She sat down beside him and propped her feet upon a chair. "Now, who is this one, coming into my home reeking of true love?"

"Just a girl," replied the Woodcutter.

"Just a girl, you say," said Baba Yaga. "I wasn't born yesterday. Just a girl wouldn't demand a night with the Prince for a day's wage. Just a girl couldn't have finished all my sewing."

The Woodcutter shrugged and then said as he tapped out his pipe, "She said that the Prince slept soundly and she could not wake him. Would you know why?"

Baba Yaga gave him a wink. "I haven't a clue."

"Why do you consort with the Queen and the Gentleman?" the Woodcutter chided.

Baba Yaga got up. "What do you know? You, who come waltzing in here with a pretty girl and a pipe of smoke? You, who have a house that stands still?"

"So they said you could keep your castle here if you helped them?" asked the Woodcutter.

"Bah. Why don't you ask them? They'll be here soon enough," said Baba Yaga.

The Woodcutter did not let her see the emotions that coursed through his chest.

"How soon?" he asked.

"In time for the wedding." Baba Yaga leered toward him. "Your face looks as if a bone were stuck in your throat, Woodcutter. I don't play sides. A bargain is a bargain, and I have made a bargain with the Queen and her Gentleman."

"What about a bargain with me?" asked the Woodcutter.

Baba Yaga chuckled. "A bargain with you? I suppose I have a mountain of rice and wheat you could sort or a quest to get a devil's hair I could send you upon, but it won't do you any good. I have given my word."

The Woodcutter held up his hand. "I do not ask you to break a binding. I ask only you not to tell the Queen or the Gentleman we are here, nor hinder us in our actions."

Baba Yaga sat back down before him. "And what do you offer me if I should agree to such terms?"

The Woodcutter puffed his pipe before speaking. "Do roses grow here at the castle?"

Baba Yaga's face grew pale. "Indeed they do."

Baba Yaga and the Woodcutter stood in the garden of the Prince's palace, a short walk away.

She licked her lips and watched the Woodcutter as he stepped toward a rosebush.

"Get on with it," she urged. Her eyes shone with greed.

The Woodcutter placed his hands upon a rose. He turned to Baba Yaga, binding her to the pledge. "In return for this gift, you will not speak to anyone of me or Iron Shoes. If asked, you have no knowledge of who we are. You will not hinder us as we attempt to defeat the Queen and her Gentleman."

Baba Yaga nodded furiously. "Agreed! Agreed! Do your work!"

The Woodcutter closed his eyes and whispered to the plant.

The rose sighed and the petals began to fall, fall until nothing was left but the swollen ovary. The ovary opened and dropped its pollinated seeds into the Woodcutter's palm.

He walked to an adjoining bed and patted the seeds into the soil. He spread his hands and whispered a quiet request. The ground warmed beneath his fingers, and a small green seedling poked its head out from the dirt.

The Woodcutter smiled before turning back to Baba Yaga. "If you remain true to your word, in three days' time this plant will bloom a single blue rose."

Baba Yaga swayed and tasted the word upon her lips. "A blue rose…"

But the Woodcutter continued. "If you do not remain true to your word, this ground will become barren to blue roses for eternity."

Baba Yaga stopped. "I never said that was part of the deal."

The Woodcutter placed his finger aside his nose. "You never said it was not."

Baba Yaga glared at him. "I hope your seamstress fails. I shall look forward to boiling her in my soup."

But Iron Shoes's fingers flew, and as the sun set upon the second day and the second spool emptied, the mending was done so that not even a thistle could fit between the seams.

Grudgingly, Baba Yaga took Iron Shoes to her husband's bedroom for a second night.

For a second night, the Woodcutter slept in the dark of the laundry room.

CHAPTER 65

Iron Shoes returned in the morning. Tears stained her face. She had not been able to wake her husband.

"Only one spool left," she whispered. "My heart shall break…"

The Woodcutter smoothed her hair. "Despair not," he soothed.

Iron Shoes sat in the middle of the room, the light from a narrow window dimly cutting through the shadows, surrounded by three times the mending she had done in the days before. She held her head high as she threaded the final needle.

The Woodcutter slowly closed the door behind him.

He walked out to the gardens of the Prince's palace, to the small patch of earth of yesterday.

The blue rose bush continued to grow.

Baba Yaga had not yet betrayed them.

The Woodcutter found a bench beneath an apple tree. He leaned his back against the trunk and stroked the tree's rough bark. The voice of the tree was a quiet whisper, a quiet sigh that begged, *Help…*

He sat there with the tree until the sun rose to its zenith and a party of genteel youth interrupted the silence.

A man dressed in green with silver embroidery upon his sleeves walked into the garden. A woman in a matching dress hung upon his arm, her dancing slippers tattered beneath her skirts. She giggled with the ladies and gentlemen following behind.

The Woodcutter's eyes did not leave them.

The Green Dancing Lady carelessly chattered while the Prince stared straight ahead. Bored, she ripped a switch from one of the trees. The Woodcutter's jaw clenched as the sap bled from the wound. But the Green Lady dashed forward, playfully hitting one of her friends, who shrieked and gave chase.

The man just continued to walk.

He passed the Woodcutter and then stopped.

He turned.

"I don't believe you are supposed to be here," said the Prince. "These gardens are not for servants."

His eyes were glassy and vacant; his skin was deathly white.

Piercingly, the Woodcutter responded, "I am not a servant."

And he bit into an apple.

"You look like one," said the Prince.

"Merely a disguise," said the Woodcutter.

"Oh," said the Prince. He looked around the garden. "Perhaps you should change your dress so that the others are not mistaken."

"An excellent suggestion," the Woodcutter replied, looking at the silly men and women dancing uninhibitedly in the garden. "Dust so early in the day?"

The Prince shrugged his shoulders. "I never touch the stuff."

The Woodcutter believed him, believed that the Prince did not know what caused the emptiness and vacant stare.

"You should be careful, Prince," said the Woodcutter.

"What for?"

The Woodcutter handed him an apple from the tree. The Prince bit down into the ruby flesh.

As the juice trickled upon his lips, the Woodcutter spoke, "It is unwise for a bridegroom to eat or drink the day before his wedding."

The Woodcutter locked eyes with the Prince, using his power to leach away just enough of the dust.

Powerful dust.

The Woodcutter fought not to stagger.

The Prince's gaze cleared, his mouth still pressed upon the apple.

"Trust me. Do not eat or drink anything other than the apple you hold in your hand. Your future happiness depends upon it. I tell you as a friend," said the Woodcutter as the ground seemed to lurch.

The Prince lowered the apple, regarding it as if he had never seen such a fruit before. He nodded seriously. "I shall do as you suggest."

Then he left.

The Woodcutter stood. The world swayed, and the sunlight refracted into rainbows before him, the dust crystallizing the moisture in his eyes and breaking the light like tiny prisms. He stumbled, and his hand gratefully touched the garden wall. Resisting the urge to lie down in the grass, he groped along until he came to the gate. Upon returning to the mending room, sick from the dust, he fell asleep until the cock crowed on the third morning.

CHAPTER 66

He woke to her hands upon his shoulders and her soft voice murmuring, "Oh, Woodcutter! Woodcutter!"

The Woodcutter sat, his head aching.

Iron Shoes shone with joy.

"My husband was awake when I went to his room. He was awake and he knew me," she said. She flung her arms around the Woodcutter's neck.

He patted her arms kindly as his body cried at him for more dust. The bitter taste coated his mouth.

"How do things stand?" he asked.

She rocked back upon her heels, a troubled cloud darkening her face. "He has vowed not to marry, but the woman claims the throne. She has demanded a contest to defend her right to this Kingdom."

The Woodcutter shook his head, trying to clear the cobwebs.

He felt the calling.

He felt the request flow toward him.

He could feel it in the magical currents of the Kingdom.

His presence was officially requested to moderate a contest.

He looked at Iron Shoes.

This contest.

He was called to moderate the contest between Iron Shoes and the Dancing Lady.

"The spell should have been broken with true love's kiss…" he spoke to himself.

Iron Shoes stopped as if slapped. She whispered, "This is not true love?"

The Woodcutter rolled to his side and pushed himself up to his feet. He swayed and leaned against the wall to keep from falling. "There is a powerful magic in this place. There are laws that do not match the laws that once were."

"I do not understand," she said.

"The blood of the false princess is so thick with dust that the magic of the Kingdom recognizes her blood as running blue. The Kingdom must not be able to see who is real and who is not. It does not know who is supposed to wear the crown."

He gripped Iron Shoes firmly, as if to will courage into her. "Know his love for you is true. Otherwise there would have been no trial. He would have married the Green Dancing Lady."

Iron Shoes nodded.

"Has she said what trial she demands?" he asked.

"One hundred mattresses, piled to the sky, and whoever survives the night shall inherit the Kingdom," she said.

The Woodcutter looked at Iron Shoes, knowing that the woman who wore away the soles of three metal shoes and broke her walking stick to find her true love would not flinch.

"So it shall be," he said.

CHAPTER 67

The Woodcutter stood upon a dais in the middle of the courtyard. The Prince stood at his side. The moon hung like a smiling crescent over the two columns of mattresses teetering one hundred feet into the sky.

The lords and ladies of the palace chatted merrily among themselves at the bit of sport. Their voices hushed as two trumpet players announced the arriving parties.

From a doorway on the left, Iron Shoes entered. The Lady in Blue stood at her elbow. Her skin glowed unearthly in the night.

From a doorway on the right, the Green Dancing Lady wobbled in with the Queen and the Gentleman.

The Gentleman gave the Woodcutter a wink.

The Woodcutter's face was like stone. He was charged to remain an impartial witness to the proceedings and must do so until the competition's end.

Iron Shoes stood at the base of her tower. She looked up to the top, her jaw clenched in determination.

The false princess teetered drunkenly upon her feet.

The Woodcutter turned to Iron Shoes and the Green Dancing Lady. "The sun has set and the trial begins. You shall climb to the top of your tower, and there you shall rest all the night. She who survives to the morning shall inherit the Kingdom."

The Lady in Blue sat upon a throne to the left of the Woodcutter to bear witness to the trial; the Queen sat to his right.

"No tricks," the Queen whispered to the Lady in Blue.

She turned to her coldly. "You know the binding."

The Queen laughed.

The Gentleman held the false princess's hand, and when he let go, she rose in the air, rose up and up until she reached the top of the tower.

The Lady in Blue looked at the Queen. "There is a binding!"

The Queen shrugged. "It is not of my doing. The young girl has become a crafter of her own right, and the power comes solely from the blood within her veins."

The dust within her veins.

The Woodcutter stared steadily ahead as the Gentleman gave a wink and walked to the Queen's side, whistling a merry tune.

Iron Shoes watched as the false princess crested the top of the last mattress, watched as the false princess poked her head over the edge and stuck out her tongue.

Iron Shoes placed her hand upon the mattresses to begin climbing, and they swayed dangerously. She turned to the Lady in Blue and to her Prince. "How shall I ever climb such a tower without it falling?"

The Woodcutter could say nothing.

The Lady in Blue glared at the Woodcutter's vest pocket, as if she could burn a hole with her eyes.

Absently the Woodcutter placed his hand inside, and his fingers brushed against his bumpy handkerchief. The Woodcutter pulled it out and wiped his nose before placing it away again.

Confused, Iron Shoes reached into her bodice and removed her own handkerchief. It was wadded up, wrapped around a handful of fish bones. She looked at the bones and at the tower and then back to the bones again.

But as she looked up, her hands tilted and one of the bones fell onto the earth, landing upon its vertebrae.

It landed and grew in size and strength.

Iron Shoes looked at the bone and then took out another piece and attached it to the first and then took out another piece and attached it to the next. On and on, just as before, they grew until they formed a ladder made of backbone and ribs.

She placed her foot upon the first rung and climbed to the top and then placed another bone. Her handkerchief never seemed to empty. She climbed while her husband watched. She climbed with the weight of the world upon her shoulders, climbed one hundred feet until she reached the top and disappeared over the edge.

The Woodcutter's heart caught in his throat as Iron Shoes shifted to counter the balance of her leaning tower.

Iron Shoes shouted, "It feels like the mattresses are slipping."

The Green Dancing Lady laughed. "I wonder why they feel like that." Her laughter rang cruelly out over the courtyard.

The Lady in Blue looked at the Queen. "What have you done?"

"Why, nothing, I assure you. You know as well as I that I have done nothing to alter the outcome of this competition," said the Queen. She gave the Gentleman a smile. She turned to the Lady in Blue. "Tell me, Ruler of the Seventh Kingdom, do you like peas?"

Hours passed as the two girls adjusted themselves to the mattresses' movement.

Iron Shoes's tower moved dangerously with each breath.

The night wore on and torches were brought out to light the courtyard.

Six hours into the night, the false princess poked her head over the edge. "I'm hungry," she shouted.

The Gentleman shouted in exasperation, "You can eat in the morning."

"This is stupid."

"You must endure this trial. Then you can have all the food that you want."

"But I'm hungry now."

The Gentleman exchanged an angry glance with the Queen before shouting back, "I understand, but now is not the time. Go to sleep."

"How am I supposed to go to sleep on a pile of one hundred mattresses threatening to topple over at any moment. This is *not* what I agreed to when I decided to let you make me a princess."

The Queen hissed in through her teeth. "Silence, girl."

The foolish thing threw herself back upon the mattresses in a huff.

That was her mistake.

The tower began to sway. The Green Dancing Lady screamed a piercing shriek.

As if in slow motion, the tower of the Green Dancing Lady fell. It fell against Iron Shoes, knocking both towers down at once.

The Lady in Blue and the Queen rose to their feet.

The false princess's cries followed her as she tumbled down head over heels onto the mountain of mattresses.

But Iron Shoes's mattresses fell one way and she fell the other, plummeting straight toward the cobblestones of the courtyard.

The Prince gripped the Woodcutter's arm and cried, "Help her!"

"Iron Shoes has won!" the Woodcutter declared, and thus the binding was broken.

The Woodcutter reached out.

He reached out to the wind, the winds of the North and the South. He called out to the winds of the East and the West. He called to the winds that had carried the girl upon their backs.

He called and asked them to help her once more.

But the West Wind was sleepy from carrying the scent of coconuts in the summertime breeze.

And the South Wind was tired from driving the scent of coriander and spice over the hot desert.

The East Wind was too busy dancing through the bamboo forests and playing with kites and flying machines.

Only the North Wind heeded the call.

And so the bitter North Wind swept down from the mountain, sped like an eagle of ice and sleet.

The North Wind caught Iron Shoes as she fell, caught her up in his embrace and considered for just a moment that he would keep her forever. But the North Wind looked upon her lips, and there he saw the mark of true love and knew that she would never be his, and so the North Wind set her roughly upon the stone ground.

But the North Wind was angered at those who would violate the mark upon Iron Shoes, and he bit sharply at the Queen and her Gentleman. He bit at the bones of the false princess. With driving ice, the North Wind chased them from the castle. He drove them with hail and with drenching, freezing sleet.

And the Queen and her Gentleman ran.

The false princess with her green dancing shoes screamed as the North Wind tore at her hair and cut through her skin.

Only Iron Shoes, her Prince, the Lady in Blue, and the Woodcutter were left.

Iron Shoes, her Prince, the Lady in Blue, the Woodcutter, and a treacherous pea that lay among the mattresses.

They stood in the castle as it was covered in new snow—new snow that covered the mattresses and erased the trial, leaving soft hills where the North Wind had touched.

Baba Yaga stood on the balcony of her castle, watching as it all unfolded, sipping a tea made of blue roses.

CHAPTER 68

The Woodcutter stood upon the riverbank, the covered bridge before him. The grass was thick and green beneath his feet. On the other side of the river was the Second Kingdom.

There, the grass was brown and wild. The tree branches hung skeletally.

The Woodcutter began to cross the bridge.

Trip-trap, trip-trap.

His feet clattered upon the wooden slats as he walked in the cool shadows of its roof. The sides were open, allowing him a view of the water, clear and sparkling.

The Woodcutter wrinkled his nose as he caught a whiff of something foul, the smell of rot and garbage.

From beneath the shadows crawled a creature of green, whose arms were long and legs were short. His face was pocked and covered in ooze. His breath was rank and smelled of dead things.

"Who's that tromping over my bridge?" said the Troll as he blocked the Woodcutter's way.

The Woodcutter cursed.

He had forgotten. He had forgotten a troll lived under this bridge. The Woodcutter rubbed his forehead and sighed wearily.

"It is I, a humble woodcutter," he said.

The Troll looked at him and drooled. "Now you shall fill my stomach."

The Woodcutter fingered his Platinum Ax.

One last chance.

The Woodcutter leapt up upon the railing of the bridge and cried out, "You have disturbed my water!"

The Troll looked at the Woodcutter suspiciously. "What? I haven't touched your water."

"Yes, you have," the Woodcutter replied.

"You some sort of river god?" the Troll asked.

"Yes, yes, I am, and I have brought you a gift."

The Troll shambled close. The Woodcutter leapt from the railing and backed up toward the entrance of the bridge.

"Give it here," said the Troll.

"No, you must come and get it. I cannot leave the river shore."

The Troll scratched his head, knowing there was some reason he was not to leave the shadows of the sheltered bridge.

"You bring it here. I said so," said the Troll.

The Woodcutter leapt from the bridge and onto the banks of the river, pretending he was about to drop the Ax into the water.

The diamonds twinkled in the sunlight, transfixing the Troll's gaze.

The Woodcutter shifted uncomfortably as he saw the surface of the water shift.

Something swam beneath, a shape of blue and green. Dark eyes stared from the water at the Platinum Ax. The River God had seen him.

The Troll shook his fist at the Woodcutter. "I said, bring it here, or I shall rip your teeth from your bleeding gums."

"I'm afraid I must return to the water."

The Woodcutter stepped closer to the bank.

The Troll stepped closer to the edge of the bridge.

So close to the edge, he could not run for the shadows as a large billy goat charged at him and knocked him into the sunlight.

The Troll froze, his body transformed to rock as he flew.

As the Troll landed, he shattered into three large boulders.

The Woodcutter leapt away from the shore just as the surface of the river exploded, the River God crying out angrily before he disappeared back into the water.

The Woodcutter looked at the billy goat and tipped his hat.

The billy goat nodded in return.

The Woodcutter stepped aside as two smaller goats quietly crossed before continuing his journey to the Second Kingdom.

CHAPTER 69

The trees were gray, their voices silent.

The Woodcutter found it hard to breathe.

It was like walking through a graveyard.

The words unsaid hung in the air—this was the fate that awaited all Kingdoms if the Queen took power.

The Woodcutter quickened his pace.

The castle rose from the earth, gray stones upon gray stone. The forest around it had been cleared, the land littered with stumps. The road forked, one branch leading to the castle's gate; the other branch flanked the barren ground and led far away.

Upon a stump between the two branches sat a gray-cloaked figure with a deep cowl that hid her face.

The Woodcutter stepped closer, and the figure lifted her head. Her voice let out an eerie keen, the keen of the *bean-sidhe*, the Banshee.

The hair upon the Woodcutter's arms stood and chills ran up and down his spine.

"Whose death do you mourn?" the Woodcutter asked.

His heart slowed its racing as she pointed to the castle.

The Woodcutter nodded, and she let him pass.

CHAPTER 70

His footsteps were muffled as he walked to the inner gate.

There, a single man in a rusted suit of armor started at him, his face gaunt and his lips cracked.

He reached to the Woodcutter and begged, "Food."

And then he fell.

The Woodcutter opened the flap to his pack and hurried to the guard's side. He reached in and withdrew a bit of the rations replenished by the Lady in Blue.

The Woodcutter softened the bread with water and placed it in the guard's mouth.

The guard chewed and swallowed, chewed and swallowed, as the Woodcutter continued to feed him.

Slowly the guard began to drift back into consciousness. He focused upon the Woodcutter. "You must go away from here. You must fly far away," the guard warned as he struggled to stand, but could not gain his feet.

He lay for a moment.

The Woodcutter held him for a moment more. "What happened here?"

The guard looked at him. "The new queen. The new queen destroys us all."

He rolled to his stomach and began dragging himself down the path that the Woodcutter had just come.

The Banshee's head turned as the man crawled past her feet. Slowly she stood and began to walk behind him, singing his funeral dirge.

CHAPTER 71

The Woodcutter stepped into what should have been a fine palace. Cobwebs hung from the ceiling. A hungry mouse skittered along the wall, skirting the furniture that lay upended. A shattered mirror reflected a broken image when he stared into its face.

A tattered throne stood in the throne room, and upon it sat a young woman dressed in indigo.

Eyes closed, her head rested in the crook of her arm. Her red shoes were worn and dirty. They moved restlessly upon the floor.

The Woodcutter stepped into the middle of the room and cleared his throat.

She opened one eye and then curled into a tighter ball, her feet never stopping.

The Woodcutter cleared his throat again.

"What do you want? I am trying to sleep," she muttered.

"Your Highness, your kingdom is in peril," said the Woodcutter.

She flipped her body the other way and settled her head upon the armrest.

"I come to offer my alliance and assistance," continued the Woodcutter.

She looked at him, red shoes moving, red shoes dancing.

She looked at him, and through the daze, her eyes cleared for a moment. "Cut them off. Cut off my feet so that I might live. Cut them off so that I might sleep."

She held out her moving feet, dressed in the dancing red shoes.

The Woodcutter backed away.

And she took his confusion for refusal.

Her mind retreated once more into the cloud. "Do not speak to me of allegiance. I do not want any. Go away."

She waved her hand lazily in the air.

The Woodcutter stood for a moment and then turned to go.

She suddenly sat up, her head wobbling dangerously upon her neck. "Wait. What did you say your name was?" she asked.

"Woodcutter," he replied.

She rubbed her face with her hand. "Drat. They told me you would come."

She stood up, her eyes glassy.

"Guards! Guards!" she hollered.

The call echoed through the halls of the castle, but no one came.

The Woodcutter bowed. "I am afraid they have all left."

She sat upon the throne and stared at him. "I guess this is your lucky day," she said.

The Woodcutter bowed again and walked toward the door.

Then the air shimmered.

He felt the dust settle.

A shape filled the doorway, blocking the Woodcutter's path.

"I'm afraid she was wrong. Today is not quite your lucky day," said the Queen.

The drugged Dancing Lady smiled before settling back into the throne. "Oh, good. Try not to be too loud. My feet ache so."

The red slippers stopped, and she closed her eyes.

The Queen laughed a bone-chilling cackle that echoed across the room. "Guards!" she cried.

The halls were filled with the sound of footsteps coming fast.

The Woodcutter turned and ran.

His way was blocked by men, steel armor clanking. He turned the other way and ran across the hall. The castle disappeared and he was in the Vanishing House.

The Queen's laughter followed him as the guards closed in.

He was blocked once more. Herded, he backed into the corner of the room.

His fingers lifted the Platinum Ax.

He would face the River God again before he would allow himself to be taken.

The Queen called out, "Now, now, we would not want you to waste such a precious gift on such an occasion as this."

The Woodcutter heard the stones behind him slide away.

He turned, and it was too late. Soldiers poured out of a secret entrance in the wall and he was surrounded. Thirty men brought him down as he struggled, as he fought.

They brought him down to the ground as the Queen's laughter echoed in his ears, as the blows cracked his ribs, as feet hit his skull.

All he could hear was the Queen's laughter, before darkness.

CHAPTER 72

The Woodcutter's head lolled to one side.

His mouth was so dry. His head thumped to the rhythm of his heart. A veil of black material covered his eyes.

Her laugh.

The Queen's laugh.

"Ah, pet," he heard the feminine voice purr as she drew near, "I was scared I would never see you again."

He felt a sharp nail run lightly across his neck, but he did not struggle.

"Now, you aren't being very sporting. Shall we see if you might be more willing to play my game?"

He stilled his tongue, quieted the white, burning rage that threatened to erupt.

Focused so that he could ground himself to the earth…

Reached out and attempted to ground himself to the earth…

He reached.

And was blocked.

He reached again.

The earth did not respond.

He heard her laugh.

"Oh, good, you are willing to play. This shall be so much fun," she said.

He heard the whisper of her gown as she sat before him, felt the stiff satin against his leg.

"Woodcutter, such a humble pack you carry. That pesky harp that you lulled us all to sleep with—"

"What did you do with her?" he demanded. He tried to sense if the harp was in the room.

"Oh, nothing," said the Queen. "She now rests in my collection. Such a pretty thing, such a mighty enchantment in such humble hands as yours…I had to take her away, to make sure she wasn't hurt by such rough fingers."

She ripped his blindfold from his face. He squinted, trying to adjust to the light.

The room was made of stone. Sturdy wooden worktables lined one end of the room. A spiral staircase hid in one corner. The Woodcutter's pack was spilled upon the tables.

Four guards were in the room, two by the door, two by the fireplace. One of the guards caught the Woodcutter's eye. There was a disturbingly delighted smile upon his chiseled face.

The Queen walked over to the table and said, "And then there is this."

She held up Odin's horn.

"I can tell it is a thing of great power, but I need you to tell me what it does."

The Woodcutter felt her spell wrapping around his lips, forcing them to speak. "In times of need, it calls forth an ally," he said.

It wasn't the complete truth, but close enough to fool her magic.

The Queen smiled. "Really?"

She held it to her lips.

Blow it, he thought.

Blow it.

But she did not.

"I'll just save this for a rainy day." She placed it back, then came over and patted the Woodcutter's knee. "Now, you tell me where my dear sweet stepdaughter is being held and I won't make this hurt too badly."

The smiling guard lifted a glowing metal rod from the fireplace. The Woodcutter tested the knots that bound him, looking for any weakness.

"Now, dear heart, the more you struggle, the more difficult this becomes," said the Queen.

The smiling guard and the Queen stepped behind the Woodcutter's chair. He braced himself, not knowing when they would strike.

He felt his palm char as the hot poker touched his skin.

He did not cry out. The sweat poured out of his skin and he closed his eyes, but he did not cry out.

"Where is she?" the Queen asked.

He said nothing, and he felt the red-hot iron once again.

"Where is she?"

And then he heard the Queen gasp.

"He said you bled red…"

He could not operate the illusion without earth magic.

The poker was at once gone, but the wound still seared.

"Blood of clear? What make of man are you?"

"I am not man," the Woodcutter spoke through clenched teeth.

The Queen's heels clicked upon the floor. He could hear her return to stare at his hand. He could hear her step forward.

He heard her kneel and then felt her wet tongue run across his wound.

She came around to face him, licking her lower lip slowly. "Sweet. Almost like sugar."

The Woodcutter remained silent.

"Perhaps I have been too hasty," she said with a cunning smile.

"Guards," she cried, "bind our friend in cold iron. We may have a new flavor of dust for our discerning clientele."

The door slammed behind her as she swept out of the room.

CHAPTER 73

The Woodcutter screamed as the guards bound his hands in iron and lifted him from the chair. He screamed as they fastened the manacles to the wall.

"Now, none of that, you," said one of the guards as he struck the Woodcutter across the face.

The other guard laughed. "As long as you stay nice and still, the good iron won't bite you."

Sure enough, there was just enough space in the cuffs to float his wrists.

"Wouldn't want to drain a guest too soon." The first laughed menacingly.

And they left the room.

The Woodcutter shook the iron and cried out, screamed and wailed until, at last, his voice sounded like it had quieted in exhaustion.

And then he chuckled lowly.

Iron only held injury for the fae.

And he was not fae.

He closed his eyes and breathed.

Fire was his only enemy. If she had stayed with her original methodology, the story would have been different, but her greed was her downfall. Since iron did not bind him and she was not there to block him, he reached down into the earth and connected with the flow of energy.

The wound on his palm healed into a thick bark scab.

The manacle sprung open and he rubbed his wrists before making his way across the workroom. He swept up his belongings into his pack and bound his axes to his side.

He looked at the front door and at the staircase.

He decided to take the stairs going down.

A door blocked his way. The energy surged down his arms, and he blasted the wood with his palms. The time for games was done.

He strode into the room, but the sight stopped him in his tracks.

Thousands of eyes turned to him, thousands of black eyes begging for mercy. Iron cages hung from the ceiling and lined the walls several stories high. Inside, pixies hovered in exhaustion, clinging to one another and trying desperately not to brush against the iron bars. Some had fallen upon the floors of their cages, exhausted. Their faces rested upon the cold iron, uncaring of their sizzling flesh.

Many eyes no longer opened.

Beneath the cages, receptacles gathered the falling dust and funneled it into a hole in the floor.

Quiet shock took over. The Woodcutter threw his pack on a table to free his hands and began unlatching the simple locks that the pixies could not touch. He unlatched the cages and opened the doors.

The pixies began to fly out, but far too many hovered only inches away from the ground, far too many still lay upon their cage floors, far too many were too weak to save themselves.

The Woodcutter reached into the cages, picking up as many as he could. The stronger pixies watched him and tried to imitate his efforts, tried to pick up the injured so that they could be carried to safety.

But there were too many, there were too many to save, and as the Woodcutter looked around, he realized there was no window in the room.

He stood, arms full of pixies, knowing the Queen could return at any moment. They had to get out, but there was not enough time; he was not enough to save them.

His arms were full, full of tiny bodies gasping for breath. Their bodies shivered like baby birds.

He looked around desperately for help, when his eyes fell upon a familiar shape in the farthest corner of a cluttered shelf that hung above the table where he had thrown his pack.

The harp.

She was motioning to him, trying to tug something out from inside.

The Woodcutter ran over, just as the harp pulled out a large brown bag.

The gift from the Lady in Blue.

He knew what to do.

He placed the pixies down upon the table as gently as a father with a day-old newborn.

He opened up the bag's yawning mouth and turned to the room, bellowing to all the fae, "All you pixies, get into my bag!"

A mighty tornado swept into the room. Like an invisible hand, the wind picked the pixies from the air and swept them inside the bag. In they flew, one after another.

They flew from all corners of the room. They flew so thick he could not see through the storm of bodies.

When the last pixie disappeared from the last cage, the Woodcutter closed the bag.

It weighed little more than when it was empty.

He threw it over his shoulder as he looked at the harp in thanks. He stowed her carefully away, and then he ran.

He heard the Queen's voice discover his escape. He heard her howls of anger and rage. Footsteps rang behind him, so he ran toward the silence, ran up the curved stone staircase. Breathing hard, he emerged on the battlement at the top of the fortress. He was trapped with no way out besides the way he had come.

The land spread out before him, hundreds of feet below his stony perch.

His mind searched for options as he stared at the sky, looking for a miracle.

And then he saw them.

The clouds.

He put down the brown bag, and his hand felt his inside pocket, the pocket that carried his handkerchief, a handkerchief that was wrapped around several small fish bones.

He opened the handkerchief and took out a bone, placing it upon the edge of the parapet.

He heard the guards' footsteps drawing closer.

The fishbone stuck and grew larger.

He placed the next bone upon the last.

He picked up his precious cargo and stepped upon the ladder.

The ladder held.

Bit by bit, he climbed through the sky.

Halfway up, he looked down upon the castle, down upon the raging guards as they poured out onto the roof, down upon the raging Queen who stood shouting orders, down as the guards began to climb up the ladder behind him.

But still he built, the bones in his handkerchief magically replenishing themselves after each bone that he took.

When the ladder reached the clouds, he climbed upon the stone path that bisected the dust fields. He turned and kicked the ladder.

He watched the fish bones break. Piece by piece, they shrunk and fell. He watched the guards scurry backward and fall, tumbling to the earth.

He looked down upon the castle, no larger than a pinprick, so far beneath him.

There was nothing the Queen or the Gentleman could do to stop him.

He opened the bag and gentle wings fluttered.

One by one, he lifted the pixies from the bag and placed them upon the clouds. One by one, they looked up at him from upon the soft pillows of stolen dust.

As far as the eye could see, he placed their bodies. Their pinks and blues and greens became an undulating ocean of wings and flickering light.

The Woodcutter did not stop. He continued until, finally, he lifted the last pixie from the empty sack and placed it upon the last cloud.

With gentle gasps, they gulped in the life force that had been stolen. With gentle gasps, they began glowing stronger as they left barren holes in the field of dust clouds, absorbing and reclaiming the captured magic.

Tentatively a pixie lifted from the clouds and then another. They hovered, almost unbelieving, and then swooped and then soared. They joyfully sped to the earth, suddenly aware that they were alive and well.

The Woodcutter sat upon the path, the path that, once, a million lifetimes ago, he had walked to reach a Giant's home. He sat, suddenly weary, and watched that final pixie waken. He watched as it shook off the stupor and stared at the world in awe.

The pixie took off as the last rays of the sunset faded.

And it was done.

The Woodcutter looked out over the dusky farmlands, over the forests, off to the horizon. He looked down at the lives that did not know he hung his feet over the edge of a world above theirs.

And he felt peace.

Peace.

But even as the Woodcutter marveled, the light of the pixies began to gather, began to swirl and grow larger until the faces of those that he had carried to safety were level with his.

Thousands of faces shone at him with gratitude; thousands of faces opened their mouths and thanked him with gentle bell-like sounds.

The pixies drew closer and touched him, soft gentle fingers against his skin, upon his clothes, gentle hands that felt like soft wind on a summer's evening.

Those soft hands lifted him, lifted him like water, and together they rose into the sky.

He was flying.

He laughed, exhilarated, supported by the wings of thousands of pixies, supported and carried through the night, past the milky moon, past stars and shooting lights, and he did not know whether they were heavenly bodies or heavenly fae.

His flight lowered, and his foot touched down upon the earth, touched the soft green grass of his Wood.

His heart filled so that he thought it would overflow and break with happiness.

He stared at the cloud of the tiniest fae, those fae whose lives had been large enough to fill his entire world. Slowly they began to dart before him, but then faster they came so that he couldn't even see beyond a wall of their sparkling light, couldn't hear beyond their tinkling laughter.

Each touched his cheek, soft as a feather's kiss, before flying away.

He watched them go, spreading out against the sky, like new constellations playing amongst the stars.

CHAPTER 74

He woke, his head cradled in the crook of his arm.

The earth did not chill his bones, but was a tender embrace.

He looked up at the blue autumn sky, a blue sky without a cloud in sight.

He knew the wrath of the Queen and the Gentleman would be great, but their power was weakened.

He had struck a fatal blow.

Those who falsely sat upon the thrones of the Thirteen Kingdoms would have the blue within their veins fade to red without the dust. The Kingdoms would appoint rightful rulers.

The Kingdoms would not look kindly upon the false faces of the Dancing Ladies.

The Woodcutter stood and stretched. His path now led him elsewhere—to the hellhound that the Queen and her Gentleman had freed, the Beast that they had made an unwitting partner to their greed.

His heart sank.

He knew what it meant to face the Beast.

He drank in the sun as if he would never see it again.

For, indeed, he never would.

CHAPTER 75

A wind chime tinkled in the breeze, whispering, *Hush.*

He could feel the presence surround the house, the silver fear that had haunted him his entire journey, but for whatever reason, it did not materialize.

The Woodcutter pushed open the door and shut it behind himself. His hand was upon his Ax as he walked up the steps.

He had met this Small One like he had so many before her, gathering flowers in a field.

Small hands clutching flowers.

She had been going to visit her grandmother who was not feeling well.

His mouth became dry.

Golden curls against the red velvet cape.

He had followed her here, like he had all of the other Small Ones he had been unable to save, unable to help, for sometimes the fae called their mixed-blood brethren home.

He breathed deeply and turned the handle to the bedroom.

The flowers the child had gathered lay scattered upon the floor.

But the Grandmother sat up in the bed, and the Small One sat at her feet.

The Woodcutter felt like weeping.

She was alive.

They were alive.

The Grandmother held a finger to her lips.

The Woodcutter lowered his Platinum Ax as the wind began to roar. He crossed to the bed and sat next to the Small One. The Woodcutter's fingers toyed with the straps of the secret pocket of his pack, which held Odin's horn.

The house shook and the wind rumbled at the eaves.

The old woman closed her eyes.

And the wind swept past.

"You have journeyed long to meet us, Woodcutter," the Small One said.

Her voice was too wise for a child. Her eyes bore deep into his soul.

The Woodcutter took her dimpled hands in his and replied, "I have met your true mother and learned of your true father, and I am afraid that you are in danger, Small One."

The hellhound howled into the darkness.

The Small One's eyes grew large, but her voice was clear as she asked, "Will you protect me?"

Her tiny hand gripped the Woodcutter.

He nodded, accepting his fate.

The Grandmother looked at the Woodcutter sadly.

"You know what you must do," said the Grandmother.

The child reached into her basket and withdrew a small silver tin. The Woodcutter took it, staring at the shiny surface, knowing what lay within.

The child reached up and patted his cheek gently.

The Woodcutter rose to his feet.

He took the final Ax and walked to the front door.

He stepped from the threshold and looked at the trees and willed away their voices as they whispered, *Quiet!*

His fingers left the Ax, and he stood exposed to the growing darkness. He opened up the tin and threw the contents, the handful of faerie magic, up toward the sky.

He heard the Beast's panting and growling, the massive feet as they tore through the distance to the Woodcutter.

And the Woodcutter allowed himself to be frightened.

Standing at his father's side, holding the ax for the first time.

The garden they planted outside the little cottage in the Wood.

The harvest dance and his wife looking over her shoulder at him in the firelight.

The fae trapped in cold iron.

Sitting upon the top of the world and watching the lights far below.

His wife's shy smile and her hands upon his face, kissing him in tender good-bye.

The memories flashed before his eyes.

He was afraid.

So afraid, he dropped the Platinum Ax, and his soul leapt from his body and ran from his mortal shell, willing to do anything to get away.

His spirit soul touched the earth, and the sound echoed through the trees.

A silent reverberation of such depth it shook the gathering darkness.

The spirit souls of trees looked at him, their faces visible for the first time in his life.

Eyes that watched and pleaded.

His leg stretched out to run.

He felt the presence of the fae gather in silent witness.

He reached out with his other leg, and it was matched by the sound of a mighty paw behind him.

He turned and looked over his shoulder.

The Beast's vacant eyes met his, gray and soulless, knowing nothing but the hunt.

His leg stretched for another step, and he heard the cries of the world begging him to stop running.

But the light was before him, a doorway caught in the empty air.

He knew it would mean peace.

But those voices still cried, still screamed at him to stop.

And then he saw her eyes in the top window of a house.

Eyes in a house from a memory of something he'd once heard.

Blue eyes framed by curls the color of autumn straw.

He felt a mighty force pulling him away from the doorway.

He felt his feet dragging him backward, with force equal to his as he ran.

And the child's lips whispered, "Stop."

Her whisper cut through the wind. Cut through the darkness. Cut through immortality.

And he stopped.

He turned.

And the Beast was upon him, knocking him to the ground.

The creature's jaws flashed toward the Woodcutter's throat. He lifted his arm and felt the hellhound's teeth sink through to the bone, shaking and ripping, throwing the Woodcutter to the side before pouncing upon him again.

The Woodcutter rolled to a crouch and flung himself upright to dodge the Beast.

A frightened cry escaped his lips, a cry that seemed to come from someone else's throat.

His hand was at his waist and his hand felt an ax of wood and iron.

He tried to remember what it was…

Where it came from…

And then he remembered…

It was his father's ax.

He withdrew it from his side and held it before him.

The hellhound licked his jowls and the Beast sprang.

The Woodcutter slashed with his ax as he ducked to the side.

He heard a whimper as the blade struck the Beast. The blood that ran was silver and blue. The wound shimmered as the Beast snarled and leapt to attack again.

The Woodcutter caught him, flipping him over his head.

The hellhound landed on his feet next to the body of a middle-aged man who appeared to be sleeping.

The Woodcutter yelled at the man: "Get away!"

But he did not move.

Then the hellhound charged once more at the Woodcutter.

Out of the corner of his eye, as he held back the Beast, the Woodcutter saw the doorway of light fade and disappear.

Panic overtook him as he flung the dog away.

Once again the hellhound charged, knocking him down, and he landed next to the sleeping man.

The man looked so familiar.

Then he remembered.

He remembered what the hellhound was.

He remembered why he was there.

He remembered why a Platinum Ax lay discarded upon the ground.

He was the Woodcutter.

He sheathed his father's ax and picked up the last gift of the River God.

He scrambled to his feet as the dog attacked and would not let go, as the powerful jaws clamped into the Woodcutter's leg.

The Woodcutter lifted the Ax.

And began cutting down the Beast.

The Woodcutter cut the hellhound like the tree he had never felled. He cut the Beast with a magical Ax that could never take away life.

It was an Ax that, instead, gave life.

With each stroke, the dog became smaller, began shrinking in size. The blue-silver blood evaporated into the air, and with it, it took away all monstrosity. The years of chases and killings were cut away with a woodsman's precision, cut away until nothing was left but innocence and youth.

The hellhound's bites changed to mouthing, changed to licking, licking that tried to wipe away the pain.

Finally the Woodcutter stopped, and all that remained of the Beast was a wriggling puppy leaping upon his lap.

The Platinum Ax turned into water and fell upon the Woodcutter's wounds, leaving silvery scars where the gaping bites once were.

The Woodcutter held the puppy hellhound, dazed and breathless.

He had won.

The puppy licked his face.

He had won.

He moved to his mortal body lying dead in the Wood. All that was left was to call Odin to reclaim this lost Hound. His fingers sought the depths of his pack for the horn.

But it wasn't there.

There was a horn, but it was not the right horn.

In horror, he stared. It did not ring of wild magic. It stunk of rot and decay.

And then he felt the energy shift.

The Vanishing House appeared as if coming from a mist, a mist that faded the trees into nothing as the Gentleman and the Queen came to claim a Wood left without an heir. A Wood left without an heir because the child that should have come never appeared on the Woodcutter's doorstep.

In a horrible moment of understanding, the Woodcutter knew why.

He understood that his child had never been born.

He knew that the Queen and the Gentleman had made sure of it.

The Beast had not been just a tool to rid the kingdoms of their princesses.

They had meant for him to face the Beast.

They had meant for him to conquer Odin's hellhound.

And now, his body lying dead upon the threshold of the Grandmother's door, the Woods were free of their Woodcutter.

He had defeated the one creature that could have stopped the Gentleman and the Queen—a creature they may have set free, but the only creature that blindly hungered to reclaim fae magic from mortal veins.

They had won.

And they had planned it all along.

CHAPTER 76

He stood, the trees screaming even as the puppy wiggled with joy. They writhed in pain as the foreign magic of the Gentleman and the Queen ate at the natural way like an acid.

And there was nothing the Woodcutter could do.

The House continued to become more and more material.

The pines became poisonous apple orchards. Manicured gardens of wisteria and foxglove rolled out over the wild, replacing ferns with tended topiaries. The redwoods merely faded into blue sky.

The Woodcutter's mortal body lay prone on the ground. He tried to climb back inside of his skin. He tried, but his hand passed through his own flesh.

Quickly! screamed the trees.

The Woodcutter knew that if the Queen recovered his body, it would be destroyed. Since he had not made it to the doorway of light, he would be forced to walk the earth for eternity.

Help! the trees cried with their dying breaths. *Help!* they echoed to any ears that could hear.

The Grandmother stood in the doorway. Her soul blurred between the mortal and immortal world.

"Woodcutter!" she spoke.

And her eyes saw him.

She knelt by his body and, in a swift movement, lifted him as gently as a baby. "Oh, child, we must get you away."

"Stop!" a voice commanded.

The Queen appeared on the steps of the Vanishing House, the Gentleman beside her.

"He is mine," said the Queen.

The Grandmother stood defiant. "Your power is not yet complete."

The Queen laughed, "A mere two Kingdoms, which shall soon be ours."

"Three," the small girl with golden curls stated.

A child of eight years should not have held the power that she did. The Woodcutter could see it, could see the ebbs of magic flow in loving currents around the one he had thought needed his protection.

The Queen blanched.

The Gentleman sneered. "We have carefully marked our Kingdoms."

The air shimmered and the Twelve Dancing Ladies appeared upon the steps of the Vanishing House. Their eyes were glazed, their skin too pale. They swayed slightly as they stood.

The Dancing Lady of Orange took a weakly struggling pixie from her purse.

Cold iron hung around its neck.

She brought the creature's leg to her mouth and sucked off the dust before putting the faerie back in her satchel.

Little Red Riding Hood spoke. "The Prince of the Thirteenth Kingdom still lives."

"Impossible. There is no prince," the Queen spat.

"Asleep, but alive, the Prince lives. Queen Rapunzel, Iron Shoes, and Maid Maleen have found their true loves. The Lady in Blue stands free. And the Princess Snow White, who is protected by a power mightier than you."

The Gentleman smiled. "But, child, Prince Jack's land was a new annex. It no longer counts. We have the majority and now hold the Wood."

"You forget my Kingdom," said the child from beneath the depths of her red cape.

The Queen bit her lip, a trickle of blue blood dribbling down her chin.

The Gentleman looked at her with a smile and then turned to the small girl. "Oh, Little Red Riding Hood, you know that we did not."

The Queen caught her blood upon her palms. Two drops. She threw two drops upon two of the Dancing Ladies.

Their bodies shifted, and they cried in pain. Their smooth skin was replaced by fangs and fur. Their flawless faces shaped into snouts. Their arms lengthened into legs. Their cries were replaced by snarls, and two wolves leapt from the stairs of the Vanishing House at Little Red Riding Hood and her Grandmother.

The Woodcutter cried and lifted up the ax borne by his father and his father's father and his father before that. He lifted his ax. He lifted it and brought it down upon the creatures.

His ax fell through the enchantments, slicing the transformation in half.

The coats of the wolves split in two and fell to the ground, leaving two very mortal women in their place.

The Dancing Ladies looked at one another, their eyes clear of all dust.

The Queen screamed in anger, "This enchantment did not come from you, little girl. Who is your ally? Who dares to attack me, Queen of the Fae by way of this Wood and Empress of the Thirteen Kingdoms?"

Little Red Riding Hood smiled. "You are not Queen of the Wood yet."

The Gentleman gripped the Queen's arm in fear while the Queen spat, "He's dead. His magic is gone from this place. He is powerless."

Little Red Riding Hood looked at the Woodcutter, her eyes seeing through the veil of death.

The Woodcutter understood what he was to do.

He gripped his ax in both hands and walked over to the grounds of the Vanishing House.

He raised his ax and brought it down. In the gaping cuts in the illusion, the Wood reappeared.

A leafy frond touched his ankle gently.

He raised the ax again and sliced another hole through the dimensions. He ripped away the illusion like a sheet of wallpaper. A giant hole now scarred the entrance to the House.

"It cannot be!" the Queen cried.

The blonde girl smiled and shook her curls childishly. "But it is. I am afraid the Woodcutter lives on a plane that neither you nor I can touch without crossing into the immortal world."

The Woodcutter cut through the stone wall marking the boundary of the House.

"I believe he has no intention of stopping," said Little Red Riding Hood as the poisonous orchard disappeared.

The Gentleman hissed at the Queen, "Stop him! He is destroying everything."

A tree of golden apples fell to the ground, replaced by a pine that reached to the sky.

The Queen pulled out a dagger and sliced through the palm of her hand. She flung the blood upon the ten remaining Ladies.

"He may have been able to stop two, but how does he deal with ten?"

The wolves leapt, and the Woodcutter stopped his work.

Flashing, his ax fell upon them. Snarling and snapping, the wolves tried to fight past an invisible wall that somehow transformed them from animals back to human.

Two slipped by.

The Woodcutter saw them through the corner of his eye, but his ax was deeply buried in the pelt of one of the girls.

He spun, trying to get to them.

He watched as the wolves raced to the child.

The child with small hands.

The child with blonde curls.

Blonde curls covered by a red cap.

The small body swathed in the red cape.

The child with flowers she picked within the groves of his Wood.

Always too late.

Always too late to save the child.

His legs stretched.

He raced.

It was as if time had stopped in the widening of the small girl's eyes.

The wolves leapt.

And Little Red Riding Hood threw back the hood of her cape.

With her other hand, she threw the flowers she held at the wolves.

And where the tiny petals touched, the enchantment fell away.

The wolves were replaced by two more bewildered girls with no memory of how they had come to the Wood.

The Woodcutter turned and sliced through another wolf as she flew toward the house.

The Queen screamed in frustration.

The Woodcutter felt the anger of the forest return with each cut to the enchantment; he felt it with each blow of his father's ax. He felt it and continued to cut...

And then he felt the Gathering.

The power of the Wood was no longer sealed.

The fae had returned.

They streamed in through the dimensional slashes to reclaim that which was not willfully given.

They streamed in with the anger and malice of an ancient race that laughed at the struggles of mortals.

They were the race that had graciously allowed mortals to live.

There was a reason that mortals began to leave bowls of cream and bits of bread outside at night to please the faerie.

It was not to keep the fae as happy servants.

It was a humble apology for any offense.

It was because of the fear of faerie anger, anger seen in only the merest sliver compared to the malice that rode toward the Queen and the Gentleman.

An army of immortals was led by two fearsome creatures that did not hide behind the niceties they sometimes wore. Queen Titania and King Oberon rode beasts with eight legs whose feet were flames, whose mouths were filled with rows of fangs, whose intelligent gray eyes trained upon the Queen and her Gentleman.

Queen Titania's face twisted as an inhuman cry tore from her throat.

The Woodcutter did not stop cutting.

The Twelve Dancing Ladies quaked in fear, but only the Lady of Orange, the Lady who held the pixie in her satchel, went mad. With the small bit of dust touching one who should never have such contact, her mind split and froth foamed from her mouth.

She reached in her satchel and threw the pixie to the ground.

The sound stopped everything.

The sound of a pixie touching the earth.

The strike rang, a booming echo. A booming echo that carried with it the weight of all the sadness in the world. A million screams. A million pains that the pixie had lifted from mortal shoulders.

That was the weight carried in the tiny bodies of the tiniest of the fae.

Their purpose.

Their gift.

All the unhappiness the pixie carried since the dawn of time fell upon the earth, fell and hung there as the pixie lay, its slender neck unable to lift the weight of the cold iron.

The Queen dropped to her knees, and the Gentleman's stomach emptied its contents upon the steps of the Vanishing House.

The Woodcutter saw the eyes of the faerie people upon him, eyes of anger and rage—and pleading. Pleading for the life of the smallest of the small, one that they could not help, because of the cold band of iron.

The Woodcutter walked to the pixie's side.

Too many…

Too many…

The pain swept through the glen, the screams still filling his ears.

His tears streamed down his face, and he placed his invisible hands upon the ring, but his spirit hands could not command the metal to spring away, for he was no longer a spirit of the earth, but now a spirit of the air.

He looked down at his side.

There was one gift that could destroy the Vanishing House.

Or could free the tiny one.

His ax.

The humble gift from his father and his father's father and his father before that.

The ax that was now his.

It would be spent forever.

But he knew.

He placed the ax against the ring, and it melted through the cold iron.

The wooden handle crumbled into dust; the metal head disintegrated into rust and time.

But the pixie was free.

As it lifted itself from the ground, so returned the fury, a fury that made the earlier anger seem like a child's tantrum.

Fury aimed at those who would cause a faerie to touch the earth.

The Queen, faced with a power beyond her imagining, reached into the pocket of her dress.

She pulled out a horn.

A horn, she had been told, that would call an ally. As it neared her mouth, the sky darkened and the wind swept, cold and biting.

She hesitated, but the Gentleman placed his hand upon the bottom of the horn and pushed it to her lips, eyes never leaving the nearing host.

And she blew.

The darkness fell in an instant.

The fae stopped their forward progression. Then, one by one, they let out a horrible laugh.

The Queen looked at the Gentleman in fear.

From the sky came the sound of dogs baying and thunderous footsteps. The trees cried, *Stay to the middle of the road!*

The Queen shook her head. "No...no..."

"What?" the Gentleman quaked.

"We must run. We must run now," she wept.

With that, she hiked up her skirts and leapt from the steps, leapt from the steps and ran from the Wood.

The Gentleman looked to the sky in confusion.

Then his eyes fell upon a horned helmet and a hunt made of demons.

He turned and ran, and the Twelve Dancing Ladies took off, fast behind.

Odin stopped before the Woodcutter.

The Woodcutter picked up the silver hellhound puppy, which was now rolling in the dirt of the forest, completely oblivious to the events going on.

The puppy wiggled and licked at Odin furiously.

Odin laughed a fearful sound that made the puppy wild with excitement.

Odin gave the Woodcutter a nod.

"If you want to hunt, you can join the ride," the god invited.

You can join the ride.

His offer was to ride the sky forever…

Or face walking the earth for eternity…

The Woodcutter's head bowed as he weighed the future of infinity, when the face of a woman, humble and strong, filled his mind. He could not leave her. She was his wife, and he would remain by her side until her last breath was done. Living as a ghost with her for the few remaining years would be his strength in the endless purgatory.

The Woodcutter bowed his head in thanks.

But his feet did not move.

Odin called back to the faerie host, "We hunt!"

Lightning crashed and flames ate at the ground as Odin charged off into the night, one arm holding the hellhound puppy and the other Sleipnir's reins.

The army of fae fell in behind the Raging Host, and the hunt rode west and rode until dawn—dawn, wherever it finally rose.

CHAPTER 77

The glen was silent, and the Vanishing House faded to nothing, leaving the forest just as it had been before.

The Woodcutter stood, axless, staring into the night.

He felt the energies move as she drew close.

"Woodcutter?"

He looked down at Little Red Riding Hood, a child who stared at him with such knowing.

She held out her hand, but it passed through his.

Her Grandmother fell in behind her. "Woodcutter, your wandering soul is welcome in our home."

Her eyes seemed so sad, so dulled by grief.

It took him a moment to realize that she was mourning him.

He murmured his thanks, but only silence came out of his lips. He followed the Grandmother and Little Red Riding Hood indoors.

The Grandmother had placed his body upon the large table in the center of the room during the fight. A circle had been drawn upon the floor, barring any magic from coming close to his body, and a crossbow lay on the chair to bar anything mortal.

Red Riding Hood picked up the crossbow and carried it to the window. She sat as sentry, staring out into the Wood.

The Grandmother stepped within the circle, but when the Woodcutter tried to follow, his path was blocked.

Panic filled his soul.

He had to get to his body.

He touched along the column of power, trying to find a weakness.

The Grandmother watched him as he struggled and whispered something that made him stop.

"You have died, Woodcutter."

The words hit him like a blow.

"You have died, but you may not say good-bye to your body yet." The Grandmother looked at him kindly. "I shall prepare it for sleep. You believe that you have lost your moment to ascend to the other side, but on the third day, the door you seek shall open up once again. Then you may say good-bye without being tempted to wander, and you shall be allowed to rest in peace."

Little Red Riding Hood pulled forward a chair and set it by the fire. "Sit here, Woodcutter, as our honored guest."

He watched as the old woman gently undressed his body and covered it in a white sheet while she cleaned and repaired his worn clothing. He rocked in the chair as she bathed his corpse and anointed it with flowered oils. He watched as she redressed it and smoothed his hair. He watched as she lit white candles at the foot and at the head.

So distant.

So fragile.

The Woodcutter thought he could not die anymore.

But he did.

He died watching his body so close and not being able to touch it. He died from the longing to try to crawl once more beneath its skin. He would give anything to inhabit his flesh once again, anything to be able to touch his wife's cheek just once more…

As the hours passed, he stood up from his chair, resolute to return home to say good-bye. If that meant missing the door, he decided he would walk the earth for eternity.

But he was stopped, stopped for three days by the Grandmother or Red Riding Hood.

The Grandmother and child talked with him and sang with him. They sat and would not allow him to begin the wandering. They forced him to stay with his body until it was time to go.

Finally, sunset fell upon the third day.

CHAPTER 78

The sky shone golden and pink as the Grandmother wheeled the bier out of her house and into the Wood.

He walked alongside, his hand placed upon his body's chest with such longing.

The Grandmother and Red Riding Hood stopped at the base of a mighty oak tree whose gnarled roots ate the ground and whose grand trunk could only be surrounded if ten tall men stood hand in hand. There, the Grandmother and the child transferred the body to the earth.

They stood respectfully as the Woodcutter knelt at the side of his own being.

A phantom tear slid down the Woodcutter's cheek, and it fell, landing upon the earth.

The Woodcutter buried his face in his sleeve.

But where the tear touched, a small mushroom emerged, a mushroom of red with small dots of white on its cap. It stretched and yawned and shook off the dirt and then shrank back as another tear slid from the Woodcutter and landed wetly upon its head. It shook off the tear like a dog come in from the rain, and where the spray of the second tear landed, a second mushroom emerged, waking and shaking as another tear fell. Around and around the mushrooms grew, until the tears stopped and the Woodcutter looked up.

A circle of mushrooms gazed back at him from all sides, a circle of mushrooms grown into a complete faerie circle.

The Grandmother gave the Woodcutter a gentle smile as she placed her hand upon her granddaughter's shoulder. "Do you think they would forget your kindness?"

A clear note sounded through the Wood.

A silver note that rang through the trees and seemed to cause the wind to laugh.

It chased the sorrow from the Woodcutter's still heart and filled it with such gladness, with such hope.

Pinpricks of light grew closer, dancing in and out of the tree branches.

A faun tripped lightly into the clearing, blowing sweetly upon the pipes that played that single note. He stopped before the Woodcutter and gave him a wink. The faun turned back to the Wood and played another tune.

The pixies were first, like brightly lit fireflies. They darted toward the Woodcutter and giggled at his sadness, and he felt it melt like a dream at dawn. They turned back to the darkness and beckoned to other creatures waiting in the trees. Shyly stepped the greater faeries, with wings of gossamer and halos of blue and pink and yellow. The trees opened their hearts, and the long-limbed dryads smiled upon the Woodcutter.

And then Titania and Oberon entered the clearing, sitting upon their carried litter.

Between them sat a girl whose hair was as black as ebony and whose skin was as white as snow. Her lips were red as blood and her name was Snow White.

Titania and Oberon gave her their hands as she stepped from the litter, giving the hands of the King and Queen to the young Princess.

Her eyes had lost the pain of losing her innocence. They held now a deepened wisdom of understanding.

She stepped into the faerie circle and stood before the Woodcutter, her small lips parted in a smile of knowing. "Woodcutter, lay thee inside thy body, for thou hast been parted from one another too long."

The Woodcutter looked at her, and in his heart, something lived.

He lay down upon his body and felt himself sinking into the empty flesh.

Snow White knelt beside him and rested her hand upon his cheek. She whispered so quietly that only he could hear. "I offer thee the kiss of true love."

Within her eyes was the gratitude of the thousands of souls that knew him. He saw them. He saw the faces of the fae, the faces of the Wood. He heard their voices as they whispered in his ear of their thanks for what he had endured, for the sacrifices he had made. He felt in his being their emotions, those feelings that words could not describe. They were here because he loved without thinking.

They were here because he was loved.

Truly loved.

True love.

And he felt her lips upon his. Her lips that held the love of a million souls he had loved without knowing it, loved in each moment he breathed in and out. Loved and was loved in return.

They had survived.

And he felt his heart stir in his chest.

A pleasant thump.

And then another.

And the Princess's lips lifted from his own, and he gasped. His lungs ached for air. He sat up, gulping the oxygen. Wheezing it in. Gasping. Tasting it. Allowing it to fill him as the heat returned to the tips of his fingers, to the tips of his toes. He felt the touch of his clothes upon his skin, and he felt the pulse beating within his veins.

He was alive.

Alive.

The tears that fell were not ghosts.

They were real.

The Princess sat back on her heels and laughed.

As she laughed, the trees overhead opened their blossoms, and new pixies flew from their flowers, born to chase away the darkness.

Snow White threw her arms around the Woodcutter, and he held her.

Held another human tight.

She finally broke away and wiped the tears from his cheeks. "Go forth knowing that all is set to right, all because of thy love on this blessed, blessed night."

She gripped her hands upon his arms and helped him unsteadily to his feet. The Woodcutter leaned against the tree, unused to his own eyes. They saw colors he never remembered, saw details in the leaves and the roughness of the trees. He leaned upon the trunk, unable to comprehend the beauty of it all.

The Princess laughed again, and again another tree gave birth to life.

"'Tis not a dream, dear Woodcutter."

Immediately he knelt down as Titania and Oberon stepped in behind the young Princess.

Oberon lifted the Woodcutter to his feet. "Do not kneel before us."

Titania smiled. "Our entire world exists only because of you."

"Did the Wild Hunt catch its quarry?" the Woodcutter whispered, his voice strange and glorious in his throat.

Oberon nodded. "Indeed. The Queen and her Gentleman shall not trouble this Wood again."

And the Woodcutter did not need to ask any more.

A cheer rose forth from the faerie host, and a table erupted from the earth, formed of tree roots and rocks. One hundred nymphs danced into the clearing, carrying foods recognizable and not, foods of purple and gold and green.

Titania and Oberon guided the Woodcutter to his seat upon a throne that had naturally grown into the shape of a chair, and they placed upon his forehead a circle of uncut wood.

The Grandmother and Red Riding Hood stood at his side, crowns of red upon their heads.

The young blonde girl placed her chubby hand within the Woodcutter's rough palm.

Stepping into the clearing came Rapunzel and Prince Martin. Maid Maleen and the Duke. Iron Shoes and her Prince. The Lady in resplendent Blue, gripping the hand of a young boy, a young boy with a mop of curly brown hair who had been woken from his sleep.

His little legs ran, eating up the distance between him and the Woodcutter. The Woodcutter opened up his arms, and Jack clung to the Woodcutter, wrapping himself tightly around the Woodcutter's neck. He whispered in the Woodcutter's ear, "How was true love supposed to find me in a briar patch?"

Music began to play from enchanted instruments crafted by faerie hands. Such was the music that blood that was not blue could have not endured it. The night was a swirl of dancing and voices. There was laughter, but most of all love, love as all those that inhabited the Wood came to the Woodcutter's side. Some spoke gentle words; some remained silent.

But he understood.

Understood that the pain he endured thinking he was leaving them was nothing compared to the pain they endured knowing he was gone.

So together they rejoiced in life.

At midnight, he looked up into the sky and stared at the full moon as it shone upon the celebration.

Something shifted.

The celebration became quiet.

He looked, and the crowd had parted to allow two nimble dryads to step forward. In their slender arms was a single, sturdy piece of curved wood.

Behind them came Titania and Oberon, flanking Snow White, who carried a pillow, upon which lay a shining ax head.

They stopped before the Woodcutter, and Oberon spoke. "Woodcutter, you whom have never spilled the innocent sap of an unwilling tree, you have sacrificed yourself for us."

Titania smiled gracefully at the Woodcutter. "You have faced even death to ensure the survival of our people."

Oberon continued. "In doing so, you sacrificed an object you held dearest to free the soul of one of our own."

"And so we thank you. We gift you this ax to replace the one that was destroyed; we gift you this ax, like the one we gave to your ancestor's father so many years ago," said Titania.

"An ax made of the same willing tree, an ax of the same mountain's ore, shaped by the same hands that shaped its brother."

One dryad stepped forward and took the pillow from Snow White. The other dryad handed the Princess the wooden handle. Snow White, shielded by her mortal side, picked up the iron ax head and fit the two pieces together.

Titania closed her eyes and placed her hands upon the instrument. Oberon placed his hands upon hers.

Their arms began to glow, faint at first, but then brighter and brighter until the light was blinding. Their lips mouthed silent words together, and a hurricane wind swept through the glade, wrapping itself around the two. The wind rose as their voices rose, and with a mighty cracking sound that shook the earth, light vanished.

The head and the handle were one, made and bound by the magic of both fae and earth.

Titania took the ax, trembling with exhaustion, and she and Oberon knelt before the Woodcutter.

The entire host followed in kind.

"Gentle Woodcutter, we ask you, once again, to pick up your ax and resume your rightful place as protector and steward of this realm. We ask you humbly and with gratitude for the service you have already given to us."

The Woodcutter rose and reached out to grasp the ax.

He smiled at the Faerie Kingdom and spoke so that all could hear. "I take my place as your humble servant from now to the end of my days."

Oberon and Titania stood up and spoke together. "May that day be far away indeed."

He nicked his palm and his sap ran clear.

He held the ax to the faerie rulers, and they nicked their palms similarly, blue blood running down their hands.

Palm to palm, they renewed their vow to one another for one hundred centuries.

The hundred centuries after that would have to worry about their own vow.

CHAPTER 79

His feet thudded upon the dirt path, the birds flying along beside him. The Woodcutter looked up at the canopy of the trees and drank in the dappled sun.

Living was still new, and he hoped that he would never forget how wondrous it felt.

Jack's hand was warm within his...His son's hand was warm within his.

The Woodcutter walked around the bend, and there stood a house he had not seen in this lifetime but had longed for every day in the lifetime before.

He swung Jack upon his shoulders, and his feet seemed to fly up the road. Jack let out a whoop of joy.

From the corner of his eye, the Woodcutter thought he saw a wagging silver tail in the brush, but it disappeared when he turned his head.

Wisps of gray rose from the chimney. The garden was ripe with the fall harvest. The shadow of a person passed by the window, a person who made his new heart beat faster in his chest.

He placed Jack down and motioned at him to be quiet as they walked to the front door.

His hand rested upon the handle, and he felt his breath catch in his throat.

He gently pushed the door open so as not to startle her and spoke, "Wife?"

She was standing by the window, the sun falling upon her chestnut curls and rough hands. Her ordinary face had been folded in worry.

But then their eyes met.

And the world stopped.

The worry fell to the ground, as did the dish she was holding. She crossed the floor to her husband, laughing and crying all at the same time.

Her tears flavored their kiss, tears of worry and joy and nights spent awake watching the road, hoping that a familiar shape would shape the dirt into a familiar footprint.

She held him and he held her, two souls that had known each other for ten years and ten years more.

Two souls reunited.

She pulled back, her fingers roughened by working the soil and tending to the garden, brushed the wrinkles and lines of his face, wrinkles and lines she had watched grow before her, born of the experiences they had borne together. She seemed to memorize each feature.

He took those fingers and held them to his lips, loving them, loving them for loving him, loving them for teaching him how to love.

He looked at the woman who held his heart safe as she whispered his name.

He turned and held his hand out to Jack, who shyly stepped into the home. His wife looked at the child and looked at her husband.

And then the Woodcutter's wife knelt down and gathered her son up into her arms.

And they lived happily ever after until the end of their days.

ABOUT THE AUTHOR

Kate Danley is an award-winning actress, playwright, and author in Los Angeles. Her plays have been produced in New York, Los Angeles, and the Washington, DC/ Baltimore area. Danley's screenplay *Fairy Blood* won first place in the Breckenridge Festival of Film screenwriting competition in the action/adventure category. Her debut novel, *The Woodcutter*, was honored with the Garcia Award for the best fiction book of the year, was the first-place fantasy book in the Reader Views Literary Awards, and the winner of the sci-fi/fantasy category of the Next Generation Indie Book Awards. Kate currently lives in Burbank, California, and works by day as office manager for education and exhibits at the Natural History Museum of Los Angeles.